WARRIOR INVASION: A TERRAMATES NOVEL

LISA LACE

Disclaimer

Copyright Notes

CONTENTS

CHAPTER 1

The outfit looked so good that anyone would want to fuck her.

Katie Briggett studied herself carefully in the dressing room mirror. The lighting in here was terrible, but it was good enough for her to know the teddy was the right fit for her body. The black lace number graced her body perfectly, showing off her curvy hips and full breasts.

Hell, it made Katie want to run her hands over her body herself, feeling her velvety skin through the thin fabric. She had tried on at least ten different styles of lingerie this afternoon, but she knew Ben would love using his teeth to rip the tiny ribbon holding this one together. The clothing would be in shreds on the bedroom floor by the time he finished with it.

She smiled as she changed back into her regular clothes and slipped out to find the cashier. She and Ben loved to have fun, but it had been a while since she wore something special for him. Sure, the back corner of her closet held a red bustier, black thigh-high stockings, a shiny leather outfit that was nothing more than straps with a matching whip, and more babydolls than she could remember, but it was always fun to mix it up a little. She gladly paid for the expensive underwear.

Taking the little pink bag, Katie headed out toward the food court. A mall restroom wasn't the most romantic place to change into her new purchase, but she wanted to make this time special for Ben, and she wanted to do it right away. Locking herself into a stall, Katie stripped down to her bare skin. She pulled the teddy back out of the little bag and slipped it on.

Even though nobody could see her, she felt a certain thrill whenever she wore something sexy. She tucked her old bra and panties into the bottom of her purse and put her blouse and dress pants on over the lingerie. Heading back out into the mall, Katie felt dirty thinking about what she had on underneath her clothes, like a sex-fiend superhero.

On the ride home, she let herself imagine Ben's reaction when she came home early. She saw him sitting in his recliner, having just arrived a few moments before her. His tie would be loosened, and he had a beer in his hand. He would see her coming in the door and think it was just an ordinary day. Maybe he would ask her what was for dinner. She wouldn't say a word. She would rip her clothes off and fuck him right on the dining table. He would like that. Then they could order a pizza and eat it while they were nude.

The first sign of trouble came when she unlocked and opened the door to their shared apartment. Ben wasn't in his usual spot. In fact, she didn't see him at all. There was a faint rustle down the hallway from their bedroom, and Katie grinned. Maybe she wasn't the only one with a surprise this evening.

Her flats didn't make a noise on the hall carpeting. She undid the first few buttons of her blouse, eager to get things started. Ben had half-heartedly attempted to close the bedroom door. It wasn't latched, and it was slightly ajar. She pushed it open with a finger, ready to catch him in the act of throwing rose petals all over the bed or lighting candles for her.

Instead, she could only see his feet and hands. His feet hung off the edge of the bed, toes curling slightly. His hands tightly gripped the waist of a naked redhead gliding back and forth on top of him.

Katie stared blankly for a moment, trying to comprehend what she was seeing. She had always heard of women catching their men in the act of cheating, but she never imagined that she would be one of them. The naked bitch moaned and tossed her red curls, and Ben gave an answering grunt from underneath her. The noises made everything real.

"What the fuck?" Katie's heart beat so fast that her hands started shaking. She didn't know which one of them she wanted to punch more. Katie had built herself up all afternoon for a hot and sweaty evening with her boyfriend. She was hot and sweaty, all right, but not in the way she wanted to be.

The redhead swiveled around and smiled but didn't stop what she was doing. Katie recognized her instantly. Her name was Laura, and she was Ben's newest coworker at the accounting firm. She couldn't remember what Laura did, but fucking Ben was part of her job description. Katie had met her once at a company party and noted the fiery woman with interest. She didn't worry about competition at the time. She trusted Ben.

"Oh, shit." Ben flung Laura away, and she bounced slightly on the mattress. She didn't even bother trying to cover herself up, giggling as her giant breasts jiggled. Ben sat up and snatched a sheet to cover himself, as if Katie hadn't already seen every inch of him numerous times. "This isn't what it looks like!"

Katie wondered why he bothered speaking at all. It was exactly what it looked like. She narrowed her eyes and wondered what she had ever seen in him. When they had met, she thought he was handsome. With fresh eyes, she could now see he was a bit on the skinny side. He had a paunch, and his eyes were too close together.

Her disgust and hatred overrode her broken heart. She spun on her heel and left the apartment without saying another word.

CHAPTER 2

Katie pressed the phone to her ear so hard that it hurt. She felt like throwing it across the room. She should never have answered the phone, but apparently she liked to torture herself. Was 'heart attack from the jerk of an ex-boyfriend' covered by her medical insurance?

"I can't believe you, Ben! How could you do this to me? To us?"

The voice on the other end of the line was doing its best to sound soothing. "Come on, babe. Don't make this a big deal. It was a mistake. She didn't mean anything to me."

"She didn't mean anything?" Katie screamed. "Are you telling me it didn't mean anything to sleep with someone else when we've been together for three years? Thanks for letting me know where I stand!"

Ben had never taken any of his mistakes seriously, and it didn't look like he was going to start now. "Calm down. You're always uptight about everything."

"Oh, yeah, sure. Blame me." Katie paced back and forth, burning a track into the rug in her parents' living room.

"Come home and we can talk about it. I'll make you a nice candlelit dinner and order your favorite cheesecake from the bakery around the corner. Everything will be right again. I'll give you a massage, and we can see where things lead."

Katie yanked the phone away from her ear and stared at it indignantly. "There's nothing left to talk about, Ben. I saw you with another woman, a bimbo with fake boobs and dyed hair. I'm not dumb enough to let you get away with it, and I'm not stupid enough to fall for what you think are your smooth moves. I'm not coming home. Ever."

"Does that mean a threesome is out of the question?"

Katie's hand curled harder around her phone. "Yes, that's exactly what it means." She ended the call and tossed her phone on the couch. It was the safest place to hurl it without breaking the screen. Katie had gone through too many phones already.

She plopped down on the couch next to her phone and buried her face in her hands. Three years of her life were gone. Three whole years of dating, loving, sharing an apartment, and picking out furniture. Three years of arguing over whose turn it was to wash the dishes and hot sex on the kitchen counter when they couldn't decide.

None of it mattered now.

Katie had returned the next day to get her clothes and books. She thought he would be at work, and she could slip in and out without a confrontation. But Ben was home, waiting for her. Katie wasn't interested in his pleas. Now all of her worldly possessions sat in a stack of liquor boxes and garbage bags in the corner of her childhood bedroom.

"Katie, can I make you some dinner?"

She looked up to see her mother standing in the living room doorway, with a pitying look on her face that meant she felt sorry for her youngest daughter. Again.

"No thanks, Mom. I don't think I can eat right now."

Her mother crossed the room, moving to the couch and sitting down next to her. She brushed Katie's hair behind her shoulder with a relaxed hand. "I know it hasn't been easy for you, dear. You can stay here for as long as it takes to get back on your feet."

Katie had been fighting back tears since Ben's call, but her mother's words made them threaten to spill over her lashes. She was twenty-five years old, and she shouldn't have to get 'back on her feet'. It was embarrassing. But she knew her mother meant well.

"Thanks. I'm going to start looking for a new place tomorrow. Maybe I can find something a little closer to work." She thought for a moment about what it would be like to finally live on her own again. There were some benefits. Nobody would chastise her for leaving her clothes on the floor, for example. "Maybe I'll move into a pet-friendly complex, and I can get a cat." Ben had never liked cats because he didn't want loose hair on his expensive tailored suits.

"There's the spirit, champ!" Her Dad suddenly appeared, and he sat on Katie's other side. "Don't let a bozo get you down. The best things in life are ahead of you. Do you mind if I watch a little TV?" He picked up the remote and clicked on the television.

Katie settled back into the cushions, enjoying the warmth of her parents next to her. She used to love being between them when she was a kid. There was nothing better than snuggling up on the couch for a good movie. But it wasn't the same now. She couldn't lie down with her head on Mom's lap and her feet over Dad's knees, falling asleep before the credits ran. No matter how much they told her things would be all right, she didn't believe them anymore.

The news was on, which seemed to be her Dad's favorite thing to watch these days. It was a sign of his age and personality. He liked to complain, and the news gave him plenty to complain about.

Katie watched with disinterest as the newscasters spoke of war, price gouging, and poverty. Then her ears perked up. "In other news, the most recent negotiations between Earth and planet Bonaan have resulting in EarthGov awarding a contract to TerraMates. The company was founded here on Earth, and our correspondents tell us it specializes in recruiting Earth women to become alien brides."

"Sounds like a load of shit." Her father waved his hand dismissively at the screen. "As though we don't have enough issues with illegal immigrants in this country.

Now they want to take red-blooded American women and ship them off to another planet?"

"They said Earth women, Dad. America isn't representative of the entire world, no matter how much we want to act like it." Katie shushed him so she could hear the rest of the story. She had been intrigued by these aliens from the moment they began showing up in the news.

A satellite had received an outbound communication from Bonaan. It took a few years to establish real-time messaging. EarthGov needed time to determine these aliens were not a threat, then the first ambassadors had to trade visits. It felt as though contact with aliens was a defining moment for her generation, and she had always been fascinated by them.

She remembered her teachers turning on news reports and documentaries about alien life, and the papers they had to write about what they might find on new alien worlds and how the inhabitants behaved.

Katie was pretty sure that none of the students had written about marrying one of them.

The news company played a clip from one of the representatives from Bonaan. "We believe this will be an excellent opportunity for both humans and the Bonaan," the man on television said. He was distinctly humanoid, with a shock of ginger hair whose relaxed and swoopy styling looked like he borrowed it from a boy band on Earth.

His English was almost perfect. It sounded as if he were from a foreign country, not an alien planet. "We are desperately short of females here due to a genetic anomaly, and it's a fantastic chance for beautiful human women to explore a new life safely. The first ships will start running in a month."

Katie felt her heart leap out of her chest. She had seen numerous photos and high-definition videos of Bonaan, but the chance to set foot on an alien planet for free was tempting. Documentaries portrayed the Bonaan as a gentle people, and their world was remarkable. Katie had even dreamed of becoming a botanist, hoping to land a job where she could study alien flora.

Her dreams had been pushed aside in college for something practical, but where had that gotten her? Nowhere fast.

The television cut to a scene of a protest march, with people holding up signs and shouting at passers-by. "There has been some backlash against the new program," the anchorman droned on, "with demonstrations arising in some of the metropolitan areas. But Sophie Lynch, the CEO of TerraMates, says no one will deter them. According to TerraMates, they are overflowing with applications."

In the background, demonstrators held up signs with catchphrases like "Keep Earth Women on Earth" and "Alien Sex Isn't Safe Sex." Katie hadn't thought about fucking an alien, but the idea was intriguing.

The camera switched back to the anchorman. "TerraMates is taking applications right now. You can apply through their website or the M8r app on your phone."

Katie jumped off the couch, sending her phone flying to the floor. She raced to the computer in the den. Katie didn't have to be stuck in her miserable life. She didn't even have to stay on the same planet as Ben. There was a solution to everything, and it was only a few clicks away.

"What are you doing?" her mom asked.

"I'm going to space!"

CHAPTER 3

Katie's application flew through TerraMates, and they approved her within a day. Her parents hovered in the doorway of her old bedroom as she packed up everything she might need for a trip to another world. They kept asking if she was sure and if she had read all the fine print.

"Of course I have," Katie assured them for the hundredth time. "They give me thirty days from my arrival on Bonaan to change my mind. Hell, maybe I'll take a little vacation, then come right back."

"Have you talked to your boss?" Her Dad had always been the logical one.

Katie wanted to roll her eyes. Her parents thought they still had to babysit her and make sure she tied up all of her loose ends. She had talked to her boss, and he hadn't been happy.

She had worked for Summerdale Finance for the last four years, starting with an internship while she was still in college. She was ridiculously loyal to the company, although she hadn't always seen it as exploitation. Katie showed up to work at least fifteen minutes early every morning and would already be into daily reports by the time Mr. Moody arrived. She didn't take extra time on her lunch break, even when the supervisors were away at meetings. She never protested about working late when other people got behind.

She was the perfect employee, and her boss knew it. But he'd already been distressed about her taking the time to deal with her breakup, and he was furious when Katie said she was leaving.

"Yes, Dad. I talked to him." She sighed, tucking a strand of shoulder-length brown hair behind her ear as she examined the contents of the suitcase.

"Well?" He prodded her impatiently. "What did he say? Will he let you have your old job back if you change your mind? Can he put you on leave instead of terminating you?"

Katie considered lying to spare his feelings. The angry words her boss tossed at her and the screaming she yelled back had ensured that Katie would never return to Summerdale Finance. She shook her head. "Nope. I finished all the paperwork, and there's no going back."

"Why don't you stop packing and talk to him again? Don't burn all your bridges behind you." Her father tried to close the top of the suitcase, but Katie forced it open.

"I'm already done, Dad. Remember? I'm going."

"I could get you a job at the furniture store downtown. Jim could use some help. I don't think it pays as much as Summerdale, but it might be a nice break for you. I'm sure you would be good at keeping the books straight at the shop."

"I don't want to work at the furniture store, Dad. TerraMates is giving me an excellent opportunity, and I'm going to take it."

"But they want you to marry one of those men." Her parents exchanged a glance. "That means you'll have to...you know... perform wifely duties."

"Yes, Mom, I know." Katie tossed a pair of flip-flops into her suitcase. She almost laughed out loud at her mother's prudishness, but she didn't want to make them feel bad. "I promise you that if I get there, and decide I don't want to have sex with an alien, I'll turn around and catch the next spaceship home."

Without any further arguments, her parents turned around and left her to pack.

Katie looked around for anything else that needed to go to Bonaan with her. With a shrug, she stuffed the black lace teddy into one of the inside pockets of her suitcase. There was no telling whether aliens went for things like that, but it wasn't a bad idea.

She sat down on her bed next to her suitcase with a huff. As exciting as it was to be starting off on a new journey, packing and worrying were starting to take their toll on her. Her parents hadn't been wrong: she was going to marry an alien. It was a crazy scheme, the kind of thing usually reserved for true adventurists or the terminally single.

Katie wasn't either one. She was not an adventurer. Katie had only left her home state of Illinois a few times, and that was only a road trip to an adjacent state. She'd never been out of the country.

And as for being single? She'd never really had a problem with men. She'd had a few boyfriends in high school and college, and when Ben came around she thought he was the one. There had never been a question in her mind.

They seemed perfect for each other. He was going to school for business management, and she was getting her degree in finance. They would be the ultimate power couple, and all their friends agreed.

When some of her friends got engaged after a year or so of dating, Katie hadn't minded that Ben was a little slower on the uptake. It made sense to take things slowly. It wasn't like either one of them was going anywhere.

And then, of course, there had been the sex. She'd had a little experience before they met, but he brought out the vixen in her. Fucking Ben was never routine or boring.

He was always wanting to do something different, like bending her over the coffee table in the middle of the day or dragging her into a dressing room. She eagerly went with him to the adult store outside of town to pick out new items for experimentation. Ben was an expert at bringing her to ecstasy over and over again, so she never said no to any new ideas. In fact, he'd gotten so used to her compliance that he didn't bother asking anymore. He did whatever he wanted.

Ben was always a gentleman when they went out to dinner or one of the numerous company parties, but the devil in him always came out when the two of them were alone. It made her feel sexy and alive, and she thought he felt the same way.

Now she wondered why he had suddenly decided that she wasn't enough. Why did he have to turn to a big-busted coworker? The memory made her relive the things he liked to do to her and how they made her feel. Her nipples tingled rebelliously at the memory of Ben wrapping his tie around her like a blindfold, and she shook her head to pull herself out of her little fantasy.

God damn it. None of it mattered now. Not any of it.

Her cell phone chirped from the nightstand. When Katie picked it up, she didn't recognize the number. "Hello?"

"What's this I hear about you flying off to outer space as a mail-order bride?" Ben asked, cutting right to the chase. He sounded angry.

"Ben? Where are you calling me from?" Katie frowned at the phone. She pulled it away from her ear and checked the number again.

"I borrowed my friend's phone. It was the only option I had since you were ignoring me."

Katie couldn't deny that. He had called and texted her several times a day since their last conversation. She had deleted his messages without reading them and put Ben on ignore every time he called. She was tired of kicking a dead horse and didn't know why he was so insistent.

"Why do you care?" she asked, not sure she wanted to know the answer.

"Because I love you, babe. We belong together. Don't you know that? Besides, I think what you're doing is rash. Come on, an alien? It's not going to be anything like what you and I have. Certainly nothing like what I have. Will he even have a cock?"

Katie snorted. "I think it's time I went and did something spontaneous and for myself. Logic hasn't worked out for my life so far. I thought you were smart enough to understand I don't want what you and I had."

Why did men have to be so stupid?

"Listen to me, Katie."

"No." She had to stop him. "You listen to me. I am not getting back together with you. I'm not going to talk about it with you. I'm not going to come groveling back to your apartment so you can turn around and screw someone else behind my back. Go have your fun. I'll be off somewhere fucking an alien! I bet he has two cocks!"

She hung up the phone and slammed her suitcase shut. It was time to head to the spaceport.

CHAPTER 4

Katie's feet tingled from nervousness as she stood up from her chair in the waiting area and headed down the ramp leading to the ship. "It's just like getting on an airplane," she whispered to herself. She still had to get her ticket, go through security, and wait in a hard plastic chair until the announcer called her number. There was still a long, covered corridor that led down to the side of the spaceship. Some things never changed.

Commercial flights into space had run for a few years now, but deep down she knew she was leaving Earth behind, and it was nothing like a plane ride. At least none of the demonstrators from television had bothered to block the entrance to the interstellar spaceport.

She stepped onto the ship, and it had a slightly familiar smell of new plastic and antiseptic wash. The women were allowed to pick their seats, and Katie chose one next to the window on the left side of the vessel which would allow her to photograph the view as her flight departed. She had promised her mother she would be careful, but Katie promised her father to send back plenty of pictures of space, the ship, the aliens, and the food.

"Welcome to the TerraMates Transport System, flight 2330. Please secure your carry-on luggage in the overhead compartments and fasten your safety belts," said a pleasant voice over the speaker. "We will be taking off as soon as possible."

Two women slightly younger than Katie eagerly plopped down in the seats next to her. "I can't wait to get there," said the one on the outside, a blonde with massive cleavage. "This is going to be romantic."

"I sure hope so," replied her friend. The second woman had put up her short brown hair in a glossy bob. "If it's not, I might miss what I'm leaving behind."

"Who, Bobby?" the blonde asked.

The brunette shook her head. "Nope, all of his friends!"

The two girls cackled for a minute before they finally caught their breath. "Seriously, though," said the blonde, putting a thoughtful finger against one pink lip, "I wonder what these alien men are going to be like. All the brochures said they're similar to humans, but I want to know what they look like downstairs."

"Wouldn't it be crazy to find out they had blue cocks or something?" The brunette giggled. "What if they like to have sex in public?" The two hooted like flying off to marry an alien was nothing more than a sorority party to them. It made Katie feel old. It also made her wonder what exactly she had signed herself up for.

According to the contract, the Bonaan engagements were different than typical TerraMates marriages. TerraMates would match her with a Bonaan male by the time she arrived. Couples were paired up according to their answers to survey questions. But information about how many children she wanted and if she smoked wouldn't necessarily mean two people would be attracted to each other. What if she traveled all the way across the galaxy and discovered her 'perfect match' was merely an exotic version of Ben?

Then again, it could be incredible. She leaned back against the headrest and stared out the window, letting herself fantasize. She imagined stepping into the Bonaan spaceport, looking around nervously for the right place to go. A handsome man, strong and gentle, would push his way out of the crowd and introduce himself. He would give her a flower, not a rose but some other romantic bloom indigenous to Bonaan. Something that glowed in the dark.

She thought about their eyes locking and seeing him overcome with animal lust. Maybe he was in heat. He would scoop her up in muscular arms and carry her back to his place, where they would make hot, not-public, not-blue, not-weird love. When they finished, she would lie next to him in his alien bed, and they would talk, realizing just how much they had in common.

He wouldn't want to wait to get married. He would love cats or the Bonaan equivalent. He wouldn't let her fall in love with him and betray her years into their relationship. Instead, he would introduce her to all of his friends and family members and get excited when they made a trip back to Earth to visit the humans.

Her perfect man would be an alien.

It was an alluring fantasy, and one she'd already had plenty of times about human males. But it never got old and always left her with a tingling between her legs that she shouldn't feel in public.

The engines roared to life, and Katie felt her seat rumble underneath her. It would have increased her pleasure if she wasn't about to throw herself on the mercy of extraterrestrials. The force of the ship pressed her back into her seat, making it hard to turn her head. Fortunately, she was fascinated by what she saw out the window.

The buildings around the spaceport on the east side of town came swiftly into view before they began to shrink. The entire city looked like a picture book before she knew it, the cars and people rapidly disappearing, leaving only larger elements visible.

A river ran through the map below her like a snake, shiny and glorious. Even the bodies of water slowly dissipated into a misty haze indicating the ship was headed into the clouds. Where a terrestrial flight would have leveled out, the spaceship kept moving, heading up to a place where the sky turned from a darker shade of blue into inky darkness.

CHAPTER 5

Troxeo slid his thumb against the yoke of his ship. Switches, buttons, lights, and levers covered the panel in front of him. He knew them all instinctively. His fingers longed to reach out and flick them, to do something active instead of sitting idle, but he couldn't risk getting distracted.

The ships filled with potential brides would be coming his way soon. They wouldn't see him because he had engaged the ship's stealth mode long ago.

The sun was too bright here, even though he was far away from Earth's atmosphere. The locals might worship the big star, but it was harsh and unforgiving compared to the gentle warmth that radiated from the sun back on Oretoz.

"Here they come." Arkhan occupied the copilot's seat next to him and pointed at some tiny black dots in the distance. Arkhan was his cousin, but anyone could easily mistake the two of them for brothers.

Troxeo's hair was a light blonde, cropped short and set off by his green eyes. Arkhan had chosen to grow his dark hair out longer until he could pull it into a short club at the base of his neck. It matched his brown eyes perfectly and made it easy to distinguish between the two men. They both had the strong jaw lines and chiseled cheekbones of their grandfather. They had followed in his footsteps as enlisted soldiers.

"Let's take our time," Troxeo said. "The Earth ships are unarmed, but I don't want to alert them and risk having the others turn back. We have four vessels to choose from, and I think the last one is best."

"Is that how many they're sending?" Arkhan gave a little whistle. "That's an awful lot of wives."

Troxeo snorted. "I guess those idiots on Bonaan don't have the balls to get mates for themselves. They have to resort to importing puny beasts from another planet to satisfy their lust."

"Well, you never know." Arkhan shrugged. "I've heard Earth women aren't that different from ourselves. Physically, anyway. Maybe you should order one. Settling down would do you good."

Troxeo shot his cousin a derisive look. "Then who would command my ship? You? I think I'll pass." He watched the black dots slowly grow bigger against the backdrop of Earth and turn into spaceships. At this distance, it looked like they were traveling next to each other, but he knew better than to be fooled by an optical illusion. There would be just enough space between them to insert his ship.

"You sure you don't want to grab the first one and get it over with?" Arkhan's dark eyes held fast on the approaching figures. "We could probably haul the whole ship back to Oretoz if you want."

Troxeo shook his head. "They asked for one human and one human only. With my luck, bringing back a whole ship of them will be interpreted as carelessness instead of going above and beyond the call of duty. Just be patient. I want the last one, and I'll get it."

The first Earth ship zoomed by, completely unaware of Arkhan and Troxeo's presence. Their small ship shuddered in the shock wave and slowly stabilized. It was followed almost immediately by a second ship.

"Are you sure we have to wait? What if something happens and the last one explodes? You never know how things will go with a primitive culture."

"I can see it coming right now," Troxeo replied. "The last one is the only one I want. Trust me. I've been planning this for a long time."

The third ship roared by, and Troxeo studied its sleek form carefully. The communication satellites from Earth had been quite generous with their information, including diagrams, photographs, and even operational instructions for the Earth vessels. They were well-engineered even if they lacked the sleek designs of the Oretoz builders. Nevertheless, he knew exactly where all the entrances were on the ship.

Troxeo had begun planning this mission from the moment his commander gave him the orders.

* * *

They called him to the Innermost Chamber of the Oretoz Capital Fortress in the middle of the night.

Troxeo answered the call with efficiency and without protests.

The leaders reserved midnight meetings for the most important of government actions. During those hours, the secretaries and other administrative personnel were at home. They were also the kinds of meetings that led to promotions once the assignment was complete.

When Troxeo had arrived, Commander Reck was looking at digital maps and charts spread out before him. Troxeo had recognized Earth even before his commander spoke; it was a favorite source of controversy on Oretoz. Since Bonaan was close to Oretoz, they had watched the communication to Earth with the utmost scrutiny.

Commander Reck and the other government officials had been considering invading Bonaan for years, once the weapons, ships, and soldiers were in place. But the prospect of assimilating Earth was more tantalizing.

For one thing, it had more resources. The Oretoz could get a staggering amount of energy from its vast saltwater oceans. Earth's inhabitants were also technologically inferior to the Bonaan, and the consensus was it would be easier to invade Earth despite the distance. As far as Troxeo knew, however, no one had reached a final decision.

Commander Reck spoke as soon as he entered the room. "I have a top secret mission for you. I've considered all of my best soldiers, and you are the only one I can trust with the job."

"Yes, sir."

"I need you to go to Earth and bring back a human. I don't want one of these egghead scientists that think they know everything about the universe. I don't need someone to tell me about their environment or their weapons systems. They're so stupid that they broadcast that information unencrypted. I want to see one in person. I want to talk to it. Can we communicate with them? What are they like? The average human will give me a better idea of what I'm dealing with than any ambassador or hand-picked diplomat."

Commander Reck leaned over his maps thoughtfully. "Take time to plan, but I want you to leave as soon as possible."

Several other council members were in the Innermost Chamber as well, hovering quietly in the background. They didn't bother hiding the disgust from their faces as they watched the conversation.

"I must once again advise against this move, sir," a tall, lanky man at the back finally said. His drew the ends of his words out slowly like something sticky covered them. By his willowy build, it was evident that he wasn't a soldier.

Troxeo instantly resented him.

"It's true we don't know much about the...humans." He made a face as though the word left a bad taste on his tongue. "What if the one Troxeo brings back is smarter than we imagined? What if it escapes and warns the rest of its race? The last thing we want is for Earth to prepare for our arrival."

Commander Reck laughed. "That is exactly my point, Councilman Keyb. We don't want to underestimate them, no matter how primitive they may be. But I'm not worried about a single human, even if it did escape. It could never be smart enough to disable the genetic weapons I have prepared."

Councilman Keyb nodded, but Troxeo could tell by the glitter in his eyes that he still didn't agree with Reck. "Very good, sir."

Reck turned back to Troxeo, patiently waiting for his response.

Troxeo bowed slightly. It was little more than a nod and included his shoulders. "It will be my honor to accept this mission and my glory to die in the pursuit of it."

"Excellent." Reck dismissed him with a flick of his fingers.

* * *

Now, as the fourth ship loomed larger in his sight, he increased the power to his engines. By the time the Earth spaceship flew past, he was already building up speed and beginning pursuit. He smiled. The pilots would never know what hit them.

"How will you know which one to pick?" Arkhan watched Troxeo unbuckle his seat belt.

Troxeo paused to look his cousin in the eye. “I’ll know.”

CHAPTER 6

"Let me off! Let me off of this god-forsaken flying death trap!" A woman sitting a few rows back had begun to whimper as the spaceship left Earth's gravity well. The ride had been relatively smooth at first, but it had done nothing to calm her down.

Katie could hear the woman's breathing as she puffed and squealed in her seat. The attendants, like the passengers, were restricted by their safety belts until they reached the darkness of space waiting for them on the other side of the atmosphere.

"Will you shut up?" A blonde girl a couple of seats away angrily glared over her shoulder. "You can't get out of here unless you're willing to float out into space and die, so you're going to have to get over it."

Katie peeked at the blonde out of the corner of her eye. She wasn't wrong, but she didn't have to be quite so rude about it. She was sure most of them were uncomfortable. The Earth Aviation Administration usually restricted commercial flights into space to celebrities, government authorities, and the uber-rich. It wasn't likely that any of them were on this flight.

"It will be all right," said a calm voice closer to the woman who was panicking. "Why don't you tell me a little bit about yourself?"

The two women began speaking in low voices, and the passengers breathed a collective sigh of relief. It was hard enough to watch Earth slowly shrink below them without someone yelling about it.

The brunette turned to Katie. "So, what's your story? Why are you here?"

She shrugged. "My rotten boyfriend cheated on me. I guess it was a bit of a sudden decision, but I was ready for a change."

The other girl nodded sagely. "Girl, I hear you. I was sick and tired of all those stupid college boys. I mean, I'm all in for a good time, but they're just so immature, you know?" She chomped loudly on a piece of gum and rolled her eyes up toward the off-white ceiling as she thought. "I wonder if these aliens know anything about commitment or cheating or anything. I mean, I know we're going here to marry them, but what does marriage mean to an alien? Is it just a mating thing, or are you together for life?"

Katie, surprised by the philosophy coming out of the young girl's mouth and started to reply, but the blonde interrupted her.

"Who cares? All I know is that we're getting laid!" She snorted a loud laugh that echoed throughout the cabin.

Katie prepared herself for another conversation about extraterrestrial genitalia, but it didn't come. Instead, the passengers were silenced by a shaking that pulsed down the ship. The lights blinked off for just a moment before they flickered back on again. The woman a few rows back, who had been momentarily calmed by the chatterbox next to her, let out a bloodcurdling scream.

"It's probably just turbulence," Katie said casually to her neighbor, trying to assure herself in the process. Was there turbulence in space? There wasn't any air, right? How far did they have to get past the atmosphere before they were gliding along smoothly like the people in Star Wars?

The lights flickered again. A loud crashing noise came from the back of the ship. Katie stiffened in her seat, all the muscles in her body tensing. Another crash rang through the air. Katie tried to look over her shoulder, but the backs of the seats were too high for her to see anything.

"What the hell was that?" the blonde whispered, losing all of her carefree attitude in an instant. The other women were murmuring in a susurrus of panic.

A voice boomed from the front of the plane. "Silence!"

Katie looked up to see a tall man filling the doorway that led from the pilot's area to the passenger compartment. His wide shoulders bulged out into muscular arms that were at least as thick as her waist, and they were well-displayed in a sleeveless shirt. The rugged green pants he wore over heavy boots made Katie think about someone from an overdone action movie. He had several weapons strapped to his back, but he didn't reach for any of them. Blonde hair was trimmed so tightly to his head on the sides that she could see his scalp. Green eyes glittered out of a square, angular face as he surveyed the passengers before him.

Despite the newcomer's commandment, no one was quiet. Most of the passengers started screaming. Katie was vaguely aware of the cacophony that surrounded her, but no cries of terror fell from her mouth. Instead, she instantly became aware of every part of her body. Her vision seemed to sharpen suddenly. Even her nose was working overtime as she caught a whiff of his natural scent, which smelled like a smooth musk.

She watched his head slowly swivel, surveying the starship. Part of her wanted his eyes to land on her and take in every curve of her body. But the rational part of her brain was on high alert. There weren't supposed to be men on this flight. Certainly not a big, brash, scary man that looked like he could have ripped through the hull of the ship with his bare hands.

As she tried to make herself invisible, his gaze came to rest on her.

* * *

Arkhan had to stay behind and maintain the connection between the two ships. Troxeo was on his own, maneuvering through the access hatch alone. He was prepared to exert himself pulling open the door to the Earth ship, but it was only slightly harder to open than his own. Apparently the humans could occasionally make high-quality parts.

The passengers had acted in the way he had expected. They were a mindless mob. If he had raided a ship full of animals, it would have been the same. Most of them crouched into their seats, trying to make themselves invisible by becoming smaller. Some screamed and yelled, but none of them made a move against him. He felt like he could do anything he wanted. Troxeo found it hard to focus; the acrid smell of sweat mixed with the allure of females hung thick in the air.

He tried to study each one of the humans in turn, but it was hard to compare one to another when they all cowered in their seats. He never had any doubts that he would know which one of them to take. He didn't think he needed to know their identities in advance. It was unlikely that a significant person in Earth society would sell themselves as a mail-order bride. Commander Reck said he wanted an average human, and this was the place to get one.

It didn't take long for one of them to stand out from the crowd simply by being still. When his gaze landed on her, she stared back at him with equal intensity from her large blue eyes. Her dark hair contrasted with her fair skin and made her seem more exotic than the monotone female a few seats away that was all blonde and pink.

Perhaps her most surprising feature, though, was her behavior. While the other females were in full panic mode, this one sat as still as a statue, studying him just as much as he studied her.

He strode forward down the aisle and noticed that the female's eyes followed him. She was definitely the one.

He reached across the passengers sitting next to her, who were now babbling and crying. It only took a single swipe of his massive hand to undo her safety belt. He scooped her from the seat and threw her over his shoulder with ease.

She was surprisingly soft, unlike the Oretoz women made of nothing but sinewy muscle and pure venom. Troxeo was pleased to find that she weighed little, and she barely struggled against him. Perhaps she was smart enough to understand that there was no point in fighting him. Maybe she was too stupid to know she was in danger.

Either way, he had the human. Troxeo turned and headed back for his ship.

CHAPTER 7

As the large man advanced down the aisle of the ship, Katie suddenly realized he must be an alien. For a moment, she felt slightly perverted admiring his physique, but she remembered that she was on her way to marry an alien, after all. No men on Earth were quite that big or that scary. At least, no one she knew. This man would be entirely out of place in the business attire Ben always wore. The wool wouldn't hold his bulging muscles for an instant.

When he batted her restraint away like a child's plaything, Katie's stomach contracted. What was he going to do? Was he going to take her? She couldn't seem to do anything other than watch him dumbly.

He lifted her out of the seat and tossed her over his shoulder like a sack of potatoes before she knew it. He felt like nothing but hard lines and solid muscle. His arms were smooth rocks as they wrapped around her waist. He was so solid that he might as well have been a machine.

When she looked up from her odd position, she realized something was terribly wrong. Yes, this man had hijacked their ship and forced his way inside. Yes, he was most likely an alien. Even if he was from Earth, he wasn't the kind of guy with whom she wanted to be associated. Yes, she was currently slung across his shoulder like a girl in an old black and white movie.

But when she looked up, she saw the faces of the other women on the plane. She saw fear in their eyes, and it was because of her.

Their fellow passenger was being removed from the ship when she was supposed to be headed to Bonaan. She saw terror in their widened eyes, nails clawing at their carefully colored lips, hair that had suddenly pulled loose from little buns to stand on end like halos around their heads.

Her body and mind finally got in sync. Katie struggled against the great hulk of a man. This couldn't be happening, could it? Maybe she could do something to save herself. Katie swung her feet, but her sneakers only swiped through empty air. She hit something. Unfortunately, it was only the head of another Earth woman.

Katie beat her fists against the man's back, but her only reward was faint thumping sounds. She scratched at his fingers around her waist, at the back of his head, and at his eyes. The alien barely noticed her struggle. He continued to walk to the front of the spaceship, his arm tightening around her. She started thrashing around, pummeling against every part of him that she could reach.

As they reached the doorway, she shoved her fists into his back and pushed against him with all of her might. His arm never moved, but she heard a crunch as she accidentally slammed the left side of her head against the wall. Katie saw sparks that danced and spun, and then everything went black.

* * *

With his mission accomplished and the human female draped over his shoulder, Troxeo reboarded his ship. Even though he had never been one for sentiment, he couldn't help feeling relieved to be back in familiar surroundings. The broken lines and dull colors of the Earth vessel couldn't compare to the artistic efficiency he had come to know so well.

His ship was much smaller that the one he came from, but there was no doubt that it was far more comfortable than the Earth design. Instead of a long tube with windows and fins like the other ship, it was the shape of a sphere, making it much more efficient for space travel.

His captain's quarters were the epitome of a well-organized space, with everything he needed within arm's reach. There was even a small holding cell, which he used whenever he had the opportunity. The bridge had a spacious floor plan, with plenty of room surrounding the captain and co-pilot's seats. He dumped the human unceremoniously in the open space.

Arkhan turned his head briefly and eyed Troxeo's payload over his shoulder. "Is that your chosen one? I didn't realize it would be this small."

Troxeo moved back to his seat, trying to keep his mind off of the way the human felt in his arms. It wasn't like him to feel sentimental, and now wasn't the time to start. "She was the easiest to carry," he replied curtly. "The others were all bellowing and pulling their hair like primitives. She was the calmest one."

His cousin shrugged. "She couldn't have been too calm if you had to tranquilize her."

Troxeo's shoulders became tense as he replayed his exit from the plane. He had wanted to laugh at the human for struggling. He was obviously physically superior, so what was the point of fighting? The memory of the terrible sound her skull made as it hit the doorway made him cringe. He must be running on insufficient sleep or something. Why was he so concerned about whether a stupid animal hurt itself? He didn't bother correcting Arkhan on how the human became unconscious.

"Setting course for Oretoz," Arkhan said formally as he maneuvered the controls of the ship.

Troxeo was happy to leave Earth in the distance as they headed back to their planet. With luck, he wouldn't have to return to this region of space until it was time for the invasion. Commander Reck hadn't made him privy to all the details of his war plan, but he knew from experience that it would be quick and efficient. Perhaps promptly retrieving the human would prove him worthy of another promotion, and he would get to lead part of the onslaught personally.

As they moved out of Earth's solar system, Troxeo could see out of the corner of his eye that Arkhan had turned in his seat and was casually looking at their cargo again. "Is something on your mind?"

Arkhan shrugged, and a slight red tinge crept into his skin. "She's not as horrific as I imagined she would be."

Troxeo felt angry, but he wasn't sure why. "What is that supposed to mean?" He wondered if there was something about being close to Earth that was making them both get weak.

"Look at her yourself for a minute," Arkhan urged, and Troxeo reluctantly obeyed. The human's dark hair was spread out around her head on the floor. Her arms were loosely spread out. If Troxeo didn't know how she came on board, he might have thought she was taking a relaxing nap. Her breasts gently rose and fell in the rhythm of her breathing. Her shirt had ridden up, exposing the soft skin of her belly. Hips curved in a way he had never seen on Oretoz women. For a moment, he allowed himself to imagine what it would be like to hold onto them.

"I don't see anything special." He made sure to keep his voice flat and uninterested.

Arkhan snorted. "Me neither. She's just like all the other ones. Since they're all the same, how about you let me have this one? We can go back and get you another one for Commander Reck. He'll never know the difference."

"What do you plan on doing with it?" Troxeo asked.

Arkhan grinned and waggled his dark eyebrows. "I can think of plenty of things."

Unbidden, an image entered Troxeo's mind. He saw the human woman underneath him, writhing and moaning. The women from his planet were soldiers, just like the men. They viewed sex as another mission for them to accomplish so they could ensure the future of their species. They took no pleasure in the act of mating and didn't expect to give any. It was the way of their people. Troxeo had never questioned it before in his life. But as he looked at the soft, supple figure on the floor of his ship, he couldn't help but wonder if he had been missing something. What would it feel like to have her velvety skin pressed against his hard and lusty body?

"You're sick."

"The Bonaan are already doing it. I don't see how it would be much different, anyway. If the parts are compatible, then what's wrong with that?" Arkhan looked thoughtful. "Besides, you know the women at home aren't much fun. The Earth girls must be interested in mating if they're willing to leave their planet to do it." He looked at the limp form on the floor again. "Let me propose something. I'll take her to my cabin when she wakes up, and I'll see exactly how compatible we are. You can have her back when we reach headquarters."

"Like hell you will!" Troxeo was up and out of his seat in an instant, indignant at the thought of his cousin fucking the human.

"Whoa, whoa, whoa." Arkhan held his hands out to stave off Troxeo, but he couldn't wipe the smug grin from his face. "Why do you care?"

Troxeo struggled to find the right words. "She's under my protection." It was a logical statement, but it wasn't exactly accurate. Commander Reck had been rather vague in his commands. He wanted an average human, and that was all he said. Reck specified nothing about the human's treatment on the way back to Oretoz. If someone decided they wanted to have a little fun, it wouldn't be the first time soldiers took advantage of the spoils of war.

But the idea of someone else mating with this human started to make Troxeo feel uncomfortable. She was his prize.

Arkhan had always been good at getting under Troxeo's skin. He turned back to the controls of the ship. "Okay, if that's the way you feel about it. But keep in mind that if we invade Earth the way Commander Reck intends, it's going to be open season on humans. There will probably be orgies all over the place."

Troxeo couldn't argue with his co-pilot. Males from their planet were soldiers, and they had dedicated their lives to conquest. It didn't matter what form victory took. In private, no one would care about the public opinion of humans. He sank in his chair and ran a hand over his forehead. "Let's get this over with."

CHAPTER 8

Troxeo closed his eyes and listened to the hum of his ship. It was the only thing that relaxed him, and he certainly needed to escape. It wasn't the kind of thing he would normally care about. He was a soldier, after all. His life was meant to be spent on the battlefield, taking down the enemy either via force or intelligence. Sometimes both. The Oretoz soldiers weren't challenged by much. They accepted their missions and carried them out with vigor.

When Commander Reck gave him the assignment of retrieving a human from Earth, he never imagined it would be a problem. It should have been a simple job. Go in, get out, and return to Oretoz with his prize. The hardest part of the operation was deciding on a plan, but even that wasn't terribly difficult.

He wasn't the type of person to go through the minimum required training and lay it aside, focusing on the battlefield by day and the easy life at night. No, Troxeo spent his extra hours honing his body and his mind, preparing for anything that dared come at him next.

The human still lay on the floor of the bridge behind him. He focused on the feel of the ship's controls under his fingers, the beauty of the universe slowly slipping by the windows, and the promotion he was certain to get upon his return,. Anything to keep his mind off the figure on the floor, all soft curves and smooth lines.

The door to the bridge opened, and Chixo entered. Chixo, like Arkhan, had worked with him for a long time, but she wasn't related to him by blood. She had attended the Academy alongside Troxeo, and he knew she was a valuable soldier. She was considered dainty for an Oretoz woman, barely coming up to his shoulder, but she made up for her size with a big mouth. Most of the time it didn't matter. He had learned to ignore her.

Today things were different.

"Troxeo! What in doktan is this?" She stood over the human and studied her carefully. Chixo planted her feet on either side of Katie's head, nearly stepping on her hair.

"You know perfectly well what it is, Chixo. They sent me to get a human." Troxeo didn't bother turning around to look at his cargo. He wasn't ready to have unwanted thoughts race through his head again. He could see Chixo's reflection in the window. She had her hands on her skinny hips, and her face looked indignant.

"So you just dumped her on the floor? She could be dangerous. Or hurt, from the look of it."

"Should I care?" Troxeo shrugged. "For that matter, should you? She hurt herself. I didn't do it, this time." After he had spoken those words, he wished he could shove them back into his mouth. He wasn't typically kind to his prisoners and never intended to be. He should take credit for the human losing consciousness, if for no other reason than his pride.

"Maybe not, but she has to be in good enough condition so Commander Reck can interrogate her. You know what he's like. Even Oretoz have caved under his pressure."

Troxeo nodded. He had cleaned up some of the aftermath himself when he served in the lower ranks of the army.

"Can I take it to sick bay?" Chixo demanded. She tilted her head to the side as she studied the creature on the floor. "I'd like a chance to examine it. I'd be the first Oretoz scientist to get hands-on with a human. It will be easier to perform the analysis if it's unconscious."

"Do whatever you like." Troxeo leaned toward the console and pretended to look busy, checking their coordinates. "Whatever you do, make sure you keep it restrained. I don't want it prowling around my ship or getting loose when we land."

"All right, then. Help me pick it up."

Troxeo swiveled to see Chixo bending down and lifting the human under its shoulders. The swell of the human's breasts under the thin material of her shirt was mesmerizing. They rose and fell with her breathing, large orbs that made him want to rip off her clothes and see what they looked like without constraint. He would like to get hands-on with the human as well and perform some analysis himself.

He felt a stirring between his legs, one he shouldn't be feeling for an Earthling. If he hadn't ever had desires for Chixo, an Oretoz woman of high birth who outranked him in the army, then why should he care about a random creature like this one? Her hair looked shiny and soft where it lay on the floor. Troxeo wanted to grab handfuls of it and stroke it to see how she reacted. He wanted to probe his tongue between the pale petals of her lips. He wanted to hear her gasp with pleasure underneath him. He wanted to mount her properly, to make her his and never share her with anyone.

"I think you can handle it on your own," he muttered as he turned back around. If thoughts like these overwhelmed his mind when he merely looked at her, there was no way he was going to risk picking her up again.

"Arkhan, come over here and help me," Chixo demanded. "Troxeo's too lazy to take care of his business."

Up until this moment, Arkhan had been quietly listening to their conversation while feigning an interest in a set of digital maps. He silently acquiesced. Troxeo knew that either one of them could have lifted the human by themselves, but they each took a side of the body and carried her off into the sick bay, leaving Troxeo alone.

Once the other two had left the room, Troxeo frowned at the weakness he felt toward this new creature. Perhaps it had been too long since he had mated. He would have to make some arrangements when he got back to his planet. The rocklike women at home, with their minimal breasts and muscled bodies, wouldn't be as appealing now that he had seen this human.

They wouldn't let him caress their nipples with his tongue or waste valuable time on kisses and strokes. Those kinds of things were for the Bonaan or the humans, not the Oretoz. They would let him do his job, maybe even more than once, but that was it. With luck, they would get his mind off the human once and for all.

CHAPTER 9

Katie didn't want to open her eyes. Her head was throbbing, and it was a pulsing pain far worse than any hangover. She tried to roll over. She felt like going back to sleep, maybe even dozing through the pain until it went away. Her body didn't want to move.

A bright light shone in her face. She flinched, but it didn't go away. There were strange noises around her. Katie heard a faint beeping, a deep hum, and finally the rustling of clothing as someone moved. Giving up, she opened her eyes.

A woman stood over her, consulting a small device. She had short brown hair with contrasting red streaks that stood out from her head in spikes. Her eyes were just as dark as her hair, and they made tiny flickers of movement as she studied the screen on the gadget in her hand. Her skin was so pale that it was nearly pearlescent, complemented by the woman's tight black bodysuit.

"Where am I?" Katie whispered, glad to see that at least her mouth worked even if her body didn't. Her tongue felt dry and thick. It stuck to the roof of her mouth as she spoke.

The dark eyes looked at her. "You're in the sick bay." The woman went back to her device.

"The sick bay? Of what?" She searched in her mind, trying to remember where she should be or what day it was. She remembered saying goodbye to her parents at the airport and her mother trying to wipe away tears before Katie saw them. She remembered boarding the plane with all the other women heading to Bonaan in a search for alien husbands and to start new lives. She remembered a big, frightening man, like something out of a nightmare, wrenching her out of her seat as if she were as light as a feather.

Katie tried to sit up on the examining table, but her muscles still wouldn't move. They only made twitching movements and her body itched like hell. She couldn't lift her head more than an inch off the table.

"Stop trying to get up," the woman commanded, a surprising amount of authority coming out of her small frame. "The table has an electrical field to keep you steady until we finish all of the tests. If you keep moving around, I'll have to start everything again." The woman pushed some buttons on the device and kept her eyes on the screen. "I hope everything is still accurate. We don't analyze a lot of humans in here."

"But where am I?" Katie asked again.

"Oretoz mission ship number 2558, captained by Troxeo ar Trepniss." She spoke with a clipped efficiency like she could recite this information in her sleep. She didn't even bother to look at Katie.

Katie waited for her to say something else but when there wasn't any further communication, she fired off another question. "And how did I get here?" She felt anger rising in her toward this woman. Shouldn't she have a right to know where she was, not to mention what they were going to do to her?

"Troxeo brought you."

Katie started to ask who Troxeo was, but memories were beginning to coalesce in her mind. A huge man had abducted her. That must have been how she ended up here with this woman. She used the same name when describing the captain. Katie had a piece of the puzzle in place, but it was too small to satisfy her.

"Why am I here?"

The woman didn't bother looking at her. "You'll have to ask Troxeo. As far as I know, it's classified."

Katie wanted to scream. Not the bat-shit crazy kind of cry like the woman on her spaceflight to Bonaan. She had freaked out and demanded someone take her back to Earth. Katie wanted to yell out in frustration and let this woman and anyone else on the ship know precisely how pissed she was getting.

"Can you at least tell me why I'm naked?" Although she couldn't sit up, she could see the fleshy mounds of her breasts from her current position. Her nipples looked perky in the cold air of the room. There wasn't a way to cover herself but the table was warm, at least.

The female's dark eyes finally looked up at her again, one of her arched eyebrows rising a little. "How do you expect me to do a thorough medical exam if you're wearing all your clothing?" She shook her spiked head.

"Honestly, you humans have some weird ideas about life. But you're certainly interesting to study. You're similar to us, except more squishy, smaller, and weaker."

Katie suddenly realized the implications of her words. She must have been too naïve to come to space. She didn't even recognize an alien when she saw one. Oh God, now she was naked in front of an alien. Somehow it felt even more humiliating than before.

"I have to admit," the alien woman continued, "I wasn't sure what I would find when I cut your clothes off. Since you were on your way to Bonaan, I assumed you would be compatible with their body types. It appears that you're similar to the Oretoz regarding functionality. Your skin is thin, but it is laid out like ours. You have the same number of limbs and familiar hair patterns. It looks like the interior organs are similar in form and function, if not completely identical..."

If she could have moved back, Katie would have recoiled in horror as the woman droned on. Someone was scientifically examining her and evaluating her body at the same time! She tried to push the old tales of alien abductions out of her mind. She'd been through enough without getting something stuck up her ass. But this woman wasn't the typical gray her grandmother used to talk about, with a giant head and large, black eyes. Those rumors had been fairly well put to rest once humans contacted alien races.

"Now these are definitely different." The alien grabbed hold of Katie's breasts, taking one in each hand, and squeezed them gently. "They're much bigger than I would have expected. Are you considered deformed on your planet? Or do you work out a lot?"

Katie gasped at the woman's touch. "Of course not!" she replied, indignant. "They're perfectly natural. And your hands are cold!"

The alien released her breasts but continued to stare at them. Katie was horrifically aware of how her boobs jiggled as they settled back into place. "If you say so. But there's far more material than needed, don't you think? It's a waste. We should arrange to have them altered when we get to Oretoz."

"No!"

The alien woman didn't pay any attention to her protests, and Katie began to wonder if it was worth trying to communicate. "I have to say that your genitalia are interesting as well…comparable to what I'm familiar with, but I'd like to know more about its internal structure." The woman moved down the table and reached between Katie's legs.

"Don't touch me!" Katie screamed. "I'm not a guinea pig!"

The woman stopped, her fingers suspended just above Katie's thighs, and gave her a quizzical glance. "What's a guinea pig?"

"Read a book and find out! Keep your dirty hands off me, get me off this stupid table, and give me back my clothes!" Katie wondered if there was anyone else on the ship who could hear her temper tantrum, then decided she didn't care. Maybe someone would come to help her.

"Fine. If you're going to be like that, have it your way. I've got quite a bit of data already. When Commander Reck finishes with you, I'm going to get you transferred to the research division." She put her chin in her hand and stared up at the ceiling as she thought. "Maybe I could get some male specimens and start a captive breeding program. I'm sure Troxeo could find someone interested. It would bring Oretoz in from the outer reaches to see the show and be ideal for tourism at the same time."

"You aren't breeding me with anyone!" Katie screamed.

The woman scowled as she flicked a switch under the table. "Most animals don't get to choose their destiny, and I don't see why you think you're any different. You're our captive, and we will use you as we see fit per Oretoz protocol 22-R-14: Handling of Prisoners."

Katie sat up and swung her legs off the edge of the table. It wasn't worth arguing with this woman. "Where are my clothes?"

"In the incinerator. I took enough samples to study the material, then burned them so you couldn't contaminate us."

Katie ran her hands through her hair. "So now what? Am I supposed to walk around here naked?"

The woman shrugged. "If you want. It would make for an interesting movement study if you didn't have any clothing. If you feel like you have to wear something, you can have this."

She reached into a tall cabinet and pulled out a bodysuit similar to the one she wore. It was dark blue and made from a soft, stretchy material that Katie had never seen before. It felt warm and slightly slippery between her fingers.

As she slid it over her body, she could feel it conforming to every inch of her skin, wrapping around her curves and supporting her breasts. It covered her from her neck to her wrists and down to her ankles. In any other circumstance, she would have asked for underwear, but it was clear that she didn't need it. The outfit felt so good against her skin that she didn't even want any. "Wow," she murmured.

"Come with me. I'll take you to your quarters. Consider this your official warning not to try anything stupid. If you attempt to get off this ship, you'll only get hurt."

Katie was inclined to believe it after seeing hard muscles rippling under the woman's bodysuit. She followed her through a sliding door that opened when the alien pressed her finger against a small pad next to it.

They went down a short corridor. Blinking lights and thin metallic wires covered its walls. When Katie thought about the overbearing walls combined with the cramped space, it made her feel as though she was walking around inside a giant computer surrounded by circuit boards.

The woman stopped and pressed her finger next to another door, which slid open to reveal a room similar to the sick bay. It was small, not even as big as the room she had at her parents' house. A bunk was recessed into a wall and had a thick blue blanket covering it. Instead of being made from electronics, a gray unidentifiable material covered the walls. A round window looked out into the vastness of space. Two chairs and a small table rested in front of the window.

Everything felt sparse and spartan, but for a prisoner's quarters, it wasn't bad.

"Stay here. Troxeo will be in to see you later." She turned to go out the door.

"Wait a second," Katie said, curiosity overtaking her. "What's your name?"

The woman considered her for a moment. "Chixo." She left and closed the door behind her. She didn't ask Katie's name.

CHAPTER 10

Troxeo scowled at the tray of food in his hands. He was supposed to be the captain of this ship. He felt like a servant. A servant to an animal, no less. But the Earthling would have to eat if she was going to make the trip back to Oretoz alive. Since he was on his way to her room anyway, it was only sensible that he be the one to feed her.

It had taken him a while to decide what he was going to give her to eat in the first place. He had studied Earth extensively, but most of his time had been spent learning about mechanical and engineering issues, such as the blueprint for the spaceship taking the mail-order brides to Bonaan or information about their weapons systems.

He hadn't bothered to figure out what these creatures liked to eat. He looked at the tray in his hands and wondered if she would recognize anything on it.

One thing he was certain she wouldn't know was the bright blue bottle of epobaka extract. He had put it on the tray, and then back in the cabinet, and then back on the tray several times before finally deciding to bring it. He had seen it used in the interrogation process many times and had been forced to take the serum himself occasionally. Usually, it was restricted to more critical missions than this one. And Commander Reck had never asked him to question the prisoner, merely to bring her to him.

It was a little risky bending the rules this much, but Troxeo was too curious not to.

He pressed his finger against the pad next to the door, and it opened silently. He expected to find her staring out the window or lying listlessly on the bed. That's what most prisoners did if they were lucky enough to get a regular room on his ship and not end up in a cell.

He had asked Chixo why she was bothering to treat her nicely. His shipmate had only shrugged with a little smile on her face and told him it seemed like the thing to do. Chixo was a soldier, but she could still be too soft.

When Troxeo peered into the room, he didn't see the prisoner on the bed or by the window. He looked around the chamber, trying to suppress a small burst of panic rising inside him. She couldn't have escaped, and if she had, where would she go? Would she prefer the deadly vacuum of space to being his prisoner? Soon enough he spotted her, at the side of the door, prying at a ventilation hatch with her weak human fingers.

"Stop!" Troxeo commanded, using the same voice he used when training new soldiers back on Oretoz.

The human jumped up immediately. Apparently she had not seen him enter. She pulled her hands to her chest and pressed back against the wall, staring up at him with huge blue eyes. She shook visibly.

"Don't waste your energy, human. There will be no escape from my ship." Troxeo gestured with his head to the table by the window. "Sit down. Take a rest."

The woman moved slowly, as though she was having problems making her muscles work properly when she was afraid of him. It made him smile internally at the thought of his power, but he didn't let the smile reach his face.

He hoped his appreciation of her new attire didn't show either. The bodysuit Chixo gave the human hugged every curve as she moved to the table, revealing a fuller figure than he realized when she was wearing her clothes from Earth. Katie never turned her back or took her eyes off him as she moved across the room. She acted like an animal backed into the corner of a cage. She sat in one of the chairs and waited silently, her back curled in fear.

Troxeo crossed the room and set the tray in front of her before taking the chair on the other side of the table. He planted his elbows on the table and watched her carefully. She was still trembling and stared at him instead of digging into her food.

"Aren't you hungry?" He was surprised to hear an undertone of anger in his voice. Why did this female affect him like this? He had no real reason to be angry. She had tried to escape, but he knew her feeble attempts would never get her off the ship. Other than the single incident, she had been a cooperative prisoner. He thought his mission had been a success.

The human looked down at her food and back up at him, but didn't respond.

"You must eat," he insisted. "Otherwise, you'll never survive the trip. And starvation isn't a fun way to die if that's what you're thinking about."

Katie nodded, her hair fluttering around her shoulders. She reached toward the tray and pinched off a small bite of a bread roll. He watched carefully as she put it in her mouth, entranced by the movement of her lips as they closed around it. Her eyes flicked to him again as she reached for a small, round piece of fruit and slipped it into her mouth.

Was this creature trying to seduce him?

She exclaimed as she bit into it, sitting up in her chair. "Oh! It's a grape!"

He hadn't heard her speak yet, and her voice was surprisingly musical. Unlike the rasping voices of the women on Oretoz, it was a sweet sound. He didn't know what to expect, but it matched the desire he felt for her body.

"No," he corrected her. "It's a slopra."

She picked up another and looked like she was ready to argue with him, but as her eyes met his she seemed to shrink back down into the chair. "Okay."

Troxeo reached across the table and pushed the bottle of epobaka juice closer to the human. It was the same color as her bright blue eyes, the ones that seemed to stare right into his soul. "Make sure you drink. Space travel will dehydrate you quickly. You don't want to end up in sick bay."

She picked up the bottle and took a tentative sip, pressing her shiny pink lips against the rim of the bottle. He watched her throat bob as she swallowed it. The tip of her tongue emerged to nip a stray droplet from the corner of her mouth, and he once again felt a stirring between his legs.

"What is this?" she whispered.

Troxeo only hesitated for a moment. Everyone on his planet knew perfectly well what it was and what it did, but he was confident that the human would have no way of knowing that she was drinking a truth serum. "Epobaka juice. The people on my planet consider it a delicious drink."

"It's excellent."

She nodded again, and Troxeo had to push his hands together to keep them from reaching across the table and grabbing her hair. Instead, he focused on his training. He and his fellow soldiers had been required to take the juice themselves. Troxeo was glad he had no secrets to worry about at the time. It was hard to remember anything said while under the juice's influence.

He was beginning to realize he had a secret now that he didn't want anyone else to know. Meanwhile, the female took another drink. It wouldn't be long before she started divulging everything.

"Do you know our destination?" It was the classical beginning of the interrogation process, where he asked straightforward questions that didn't have a dramatic impact on the subject. It was the fastest way to tell if the extract was taking hold.

"No. I mean, not really. Chixo mentioned a different planet. Oz, or Orbit, or something? I do feel a little like Dorothy."

"Oretoz," he corrected.

"That's the one."

Her shoulders sagged slightly. Troxeo could tell she was beginning to feel the effects of the epobaka. She was currently experiencing the involuntary relaxation of her muscles and a foggy feeling in her brain. Although she hadn't said much yet, he doubted her speech would have been so comfortable around him without it.

"I was supposed to be going to Bonaan, though," she continued as she popped another slopra in her mouth, "until you decided to change my plans for me."

"You were going to be a mail-order bride." He tried not to let his voice show his judgment on her. The idea was absurd. Why would any woman sell herself off, especially to a race as weak as the Bonaan?

"Yep. What a crazy idea. But I thought it was the right choice. The men from Bonaan seemed nice and calm." She took another sip of the juice and looked up at him with pupils so dilated that he couldn't see her irises. "Not like you. You're scary."

Troxeo felt his chest start to puff out at the compliment. Though she hadn't sounded like she was frightened when she said it, he knew it was the truth. The juice took away all inhibitions, including fear. He wished he had imbibed some himself. It would give him an excuse to make everything he imagined doing to her reality.

"I guess I can be intimidating to a human."

"Oh, yeah," she nodded. "I don't think I've ever been paralyzed with fear before. Congratulations."

"And what precisely is scary about me?"

The human picked up a piece of bread and rolled it around in her hands, examining every surface of it before ripping off a huge piece with her teeth. "I don't know if they have mirrors on your planet or not. Have you ever looked at yourself? You're huge, for one thing. And you have this hardness in your eyes like you've seen terrible things, but you try not to let them bother you. Maybe you don't think or feel. You just act."

She considered him as she swallowed a bite of bread, her head tilted to the side. "And you've got those giant muscles." She set down the rest of the food and reached across the table, poking his arm with a finger. It felt soft and cold against his skin. She giggled. "I mean, you must work out a lot."

Troxeo fought the urge to take the massive arms she seemed to like so much and wrap them around her. He desperately wanted to feel the softness of her body tight against him and to show her exactly how powerful his arms could be. But he remained in his seat. The interrogation was going off the rails.

"Does Earth have plans to invade Bonaan or any other planets?"

She gave a little snort of laughter. "Like I would know! I don't even watch the news unless I have to. What about you? Are you planning on invading any planets soon? Or do you simply prefer to capture random Earthlings?" She giggled again.

His jaw tightened. If she hadn't been drunk on the extract, he would have sworn that she knew more than she was letting on. Was this a human way of making conversation? It had to be. The epobaka was taking care of her inhibitions.

"Did you know your ship is spinning?" she asked suddenly, squinting her eyes and holding onto the table with both hands. "You might want to check with the pilot, or activate your stabilizers or something."

Instead of correcting her, he got to his feet and came around the table. He picked her up, put one arm under her knees and the other around her shoulder, and carried her to the bed. It was impossible not to become aroused when he felt her warmth against his body. He laid her on the bed and pulled the blanket over her, even though he wanted to climb in next to her.

"Hey, big fella. My name's Katie. What's yours?" She giggled uncontrollably.

He watched her for a moment, feeling caught between the life on Oretoz he had always understood and a new life that might be completely different. He decided it didn't matter if he answered her question. She wouldn't remember when she woke up.

"Katie, my name is Troxeo." He turned and left the room.

CHAPTER 11

Katie's dreams were the most vivid she could remember having. First, she swiftly descended a twisted slide, feeling the centrifugal force pushing against her body as she corkscrewed further and further down. Next, she was on a roller coaster whose tracks seemed to be invisible. She felt every bump and gyration of the coaster cart she occupied. It tipped from side to side and up and down hills. It was the kind of thing that would have made her sick in real life.

Finally, she ended up in the arms of a tall, scary alien. His muscles were so hard they could have been made of stone, and he hefted her easily. It made her feel tiny and unique and sexy. But the dream burst and left her with waves of nausea on the bunk in her room.

Katie blinked bleary eyes furiously as she tried to clear them. She knew the alien had been here and knew she had talked with him, but that was about it. Her stomach churned. She must have eaten, but she didn't know what.

The room around her slowly stabilized. The bunk was surprisingly comfortable, and the blanket deliciously warm. She kicked it off her feet and analyzed her surroundings, hoping she had overlooked a way out.

She had already tried the ventilation hatch. Leaving through the window into space would be a terrible decision unless she was interested in a rapid death. She wasn't ready to go that far yet. The door wasn't programmed to work with her fingerprint, and she didn't know the first thing about rewiring or hacking it. Everything was useless. She was useless.

As though someone read her mind, the door slid open, and the short woman from the sick bay entered the room. Katie searched around in her mind for the alien's name. Chixo. She came to Katie's bedside and rested a cool hand on her forehead. Katie was too exhausted to pull away.

"How are you feeling?" the alien woman asked. "None of us were sure how your body would tolerate Oretoz food."

"I guess you made me into your guinea pig after all."

Chixo's eyebrows drew together. "I'll have to look up these guinea pigs of yours. Troxeo did it, not me."

Katie's mind swam around again to figure out who the woman meant. The big male. She wasn't sure which alien was more terrifying. Chixo was small, but she hadn't hesitated to lay her alien hands on Katie. It was awkward to be with her when the woman had seen her naked.

Troxeo was a terror all his own. While Chixo's interest in her body seemed to be purely scientific, Katie could easily recall the savage stares from Troxeo when he abducted her. When he looked at Katie, she felt like he was hunting something.

"He said you can come out of your room for a little while as long as you promise to behave. We have no qualms about locking you up again or even tranquilizing you."

Searching for the basis of an argument, Katie found nothing. She could learn more about her captors if she moved around the ship. With luck, she could earn their trust and take advantage if an escape opportunity presented itself later down the road.

That was the kind of thing that happened in movies. But this was real life, and she would be lucky if she managed to get away alive, much less make it back to Earth. "All right," she agreed solemnly. "Thank you."

Chixo led her out of the room and down the corridor of wires and blinking lights once again. This time, she stayed on the right side. They entered a room that made the hallways look dull. The décor of the corridors continued inside this room.

Wires of varying thicknesses coiled across the floor like snakes, biting into circuit boards and portals. Katie had taken a computer class or two when she was in college, and she had seen plenty of sci-fi movies about hackers or computer geniuses. But nothing she had seen from a director's imagination could compare to the array of electronics before her.

In the back of the room, buried behind a desk almost entirely surrounded by paper-thin monitors, she saw an alien male sitting in a chair. He was speaking rapidly and watching the results on the screens.

Chixo cleared her throat. "This is Enan, our tech expert. Enan, this is the human. You said you wanted to see her?"

Enan spat out a few more commands before rising laboriously from his seat. Though he was as tall as Troxeo, his flesh was flabby and soft. He wore clothing similar to the captain's, but it didn't fit him nearly as well. The black sleeveless shirt didn't cover the drooping flab of his belly, and his arms oozed out of the sleeves. His drab olive pants seemed to bare contain the bottom half of his body. He looked at Katie with kind and curious eyes which were the same brilliant blue as the blinking lights around him.

"Ah, yes, yes. The Earthling. Tell me, what technology do you bring with you?"

Katie looked down at her bodysuit, realizing for the first time that she possessed nothing. The only thing she brought with her when Troxeo took her from the ship was her clothing. Now Katie didn't even have that. She normally had her phone at all times, but right now it was inside her purse and flying off to Bonaan without her. She hadn't even worn a watch today.

"I'm sorry, but I don't think I have anything at all," she replied.

The tech blinked his bright eyes at her sadly, then began to inspect her carefully, hoping that she had overlooked something. He lifted her hair with a pudgy hand and checked the back of her neck. "You don't even have a microchip implant? I thought humans were quite dependent on technology, even if everything you have is outdated."

"We do. Most people are hardly ever without their phones, at least. But I don't have any of it with me. I'm sorry." She wasn't entirely sure why she was apologizing. They were the fuckers who had abducted her without warning. For some reason, she couldn't seem to help it. The alien looked disappointed.

"That's all right. I'm a collector. Even if I didn't learn anything from your phone, it would have been intriguing to see it." He waddled to a panel behind his desk and slid it back, revealing a large array of gadgets and devices.

Katie had never seen most of the electronics before, but she did recognize several generations of cell phones from Earth. She felt a small thrill in her stomach at the sight of something familiar, even if they were only plastic rectangles. The thrill subsided when Katie realized she was far out of range, and they didn't have any power.

Even though they were useless, she still wanted to hold one in her hand and have something else here from Earth with her.

Before she could ask where they came from, he slid the panel back into place, concealing the devices once again. "As I said, it's not important. Your friend Chixo doesn't approve of my hobby, anyway."

Katie glanced at the woman out of the corner of her eye. Sure enough, Chixo's mouth was curled up in an expression of criticism.

"I don't see the point in studying their technology when it's so far behind what we have," she snarled. "It's a waste of time. I'm surprised Troxeo lets you keep your little trinkets here."

Enan bobbed his head, his chins wagging. "Fair enough. But I know what you like to do with your scalpels and your scanners and your preserved bits in jars. Not all males are cut out to be soldiers, Chixo, no matter what the majority of Oretoz think. Besides, this ship would be rusting in the ground if it weren't for people like me." The longer he spoke, the more the fat alien gained confidence.

Chixo wrapped a strong, wiry hand around Katie's arm and dragged her back toward the door leading out of Enan's room. "We'll be going now."

Enan returned to his position behind his desk. "Visit me whenever you like, Earthling. I rarely get company here in my fortress!"

Katie thought he might have said something else, but she didn't hear it because the door had closed already. "He seems nice," she remarked. It felt odd to make conversation with an alien, but she might as well try to blend in a little.

"Being nice is not a highly-valued quality in Oretoz society," Chixo murmured.

"Yeah, I could have guessed that." Katie sighed to herself. This woman was impossible to befriend.

Chixo used her finger to open a much wider door. Katie gasped when it slid open and she saw what was behind it. They stepped into a room that could be nothing other than the bridge. Unlike the narrow corridors she was familiar with, the floor here was wide and open. There was plenty of room to move around. Various panels were inserted into the walls or on a massive dashboard that ran around the circumference of the chamber. Two tall, comfortable looking chairs sat at the front of the room, facing huge windows showing stars flicking by.

Katie's stomach turned to water as she watched. There was a window in her room, but it was much smaller and didn't do justice to the way they were moving through space. Katie realized with a sudden jolt that not only was she further from home than she ever could have imagined, but she didn't even have the comfort of day and night any longer.

What time was it? She had slept but didn't know for how long. Was it morning or evening back on Earth? The sun had been swirling around her head and dictating the daily routine of her life for so long that she had taken it for granted.

An alien sat in one of the chairs, but it wasn't Troxeo. This man's hair was darker and longer, clubbed at the nape of his neck. He swiveled in his chair at the sound of the door, and his dark eyebrows went up in surprise.

"I see the guest has been allowed to roam." He stood up.

Katie's stomach hadn't had a chance to settle itself, and it continued to swirl as she took in the appearance of the new alien. He had a build similar to Troxeo, in that he was absolutely huge. As she studied him, she thought he wasn't quite as wide across the shoulders as Troxeo, but he was still far bigger than any man she knew back on Earth.

He wore the same clothing that apparently all the other men on this ship did, arm muscles bulging out of his black sleeveless shirt and thighs pressing against the constraints of his pants. His chiseled features were nearly a reflection of the other man's. It was as though Troxeo's face had been replicated but with different coloring. The man scrutinized Katie with his deep brown eyes for a few moments before baring his teeth in a semblance of a smile.

He was scary in a different way. "H-h-hello," she stammered. "I'm Katie."

The man folded the bulk of his arms across his chest and glanced at Chixo. "Yes, I've heard. It seems the humans are very interested in knowing names. On Oretoz, knowing someone's name is a sign of trust. I take it that by revealing your name, you trust us?" He raised his eyebrows at her and waited.

Katie's mouth gulped like a fish out of water. Was there a correct answer to the question? Should she lie to save her neck, or be honest and run the risk of punishment? She still hadn't gotten over the way Chixo regularly watched her body, or how Troxeo seemed on the verge of exploding around her. She wasn't sure if he was restraining himself from fucking her or beating her to a bloody pulp. He kept his distance from her, standing next to his chair, but he inspected her with an intensity that made her feel as though she were under a microscope.

"What choice do I have but to trust you?" she heard herself say. For a non-answer, she thought it sounded pretty good. "I am in your care, and as far as I can tell I am unharmed."

The alien nodded. "That's very practical of you. We appreciate practicality on my planet. My name is Arkhan ar Trepniss. I'm Troxeo's cousin."

Katie smiled. Arkhan was definitely big, and he was definitely alien, but he didn't have the gruff manner that Troxeo did. There was a sense of manners about him mixed with the cold, scientific viewpoint they all seemed to have. It was like he was an English gentleman combined with an engineer. It wasn't much, but it was more than she could say for any of the others on board.

Troxeo was simply a monster, Chixo an overcurious analyst, and Enan was only interested in her for the possibility of technology. She wondered for a moment how the men of Bonaan would compare to these aliens if they were able to stand side by side. Would they seem weak or unmanly? What did it mean for an alien to be masculine? Was it the same as being a man on Earth?

"You have to understand that when we land on Oretoz, things won't be quite so easy for you," Arkhan continued. "You won't be allowed to wander around freely or speak to whomever you like. Most of us will not openly reveal their names to you. You are being treated as a guest here, but technically you are our prisoner."

Katie felt Chixo's hard eyes staring at her. Could it hurt to ask one more question? "What I don't understand is why I'm a prisoner at all. Did I do something wrong? I'm just a regular person. Why can't I go home?"

"Wrong." The alien said the word like a statement, not a question. "I don't think there was anything you did wrong. But right and wrong don't have anything to do with it. Someone needs you on our planet, and we've been assigned to bring you there."

"You can't go around snatching people up and whisking them to the other side of the universe. I want to go home." Tears threatened to erupt from the back of her eyes, and she had to hold her breath to keep them from falling. These people were obviously not going to be moved by pity.

Arkhan ignored her demands. "I trust that your room is comfortable?" he asked, taking a few slow steps closer to her. "This ship is not a big one, but I assure you that worse ships exist."

Somehow this alien easily got past her defenses. She had thought of herself as a solid stick of humanity, but he was bending her like a flower stem. He loomed over her now. Katie knew she wouldn't be able to stop him if she wanted to. "Oh, um, no. I mean, the ship is nice."

He gave an animalistic smile again. “Good, good. Tell me about your life on your planet. I confess I haven’t studied Earth life much. Do you have a mate?”

“A mate? Er...oh. No. Not anymore.” Her face burned, and there was no way for her to hide it.

Arkhan nodded sagely. “You got tired of him and threw him out of your home? Well, I suppose that’s to be expected eventually for any of us.”

“No, not exactly. He didn’t want me. But this isn’t any of your business.” She said the last part in a rush, hoping it would cover up her embarrassment.

Arkhan didn’t laugh at her. Instead, his dark eyebrows drew together on his forehead, and he leaned down to her. “Are you sure?” His eyes swept over her body. She suddenly felt self-conscious in a bodysuit that left nothing to the imagination. “You are obviously healthy and fertile.”

She crossed her arms over her body. The clothing completely covered her, but the thin material didn’t hide much. Arkhan was complimenting her in a way, and she knew that, but his words were not making her feel any better.

“Yes, I’m sure.” She wondered how red her face was.

“I doubt you would suffer the same fate on Oretoz. In fact, you might be beating off potential mates left and right. Once they got over the fact that you’re an alien, that is.”

He stood straight once more, and Katie felt as though she could breathe again. "What's so bad about being from Earth? If you don't like where I come from, I would think you'd be eager to take me back there."

Arkhan shook his head. "Earthlings, from what we can tell, are soft. Emotional. They are not good fighters. But you are needed on Oretoz, nevertheless."

The door to the bridge whirred open once more, and Troxeo entered the room. He stopped for a moment and took in the scene before him. "Take the human back to her quarters," he commanded to Chixo. "I have some business I need to take care of."

"But I just got out!" Katie protested.

Troxeo stared at her blue ones. "I'm commander of this ship. Obey me."

The door closed swiftly on Katie's heels as Chixo escorted her back to the room.

CHAPTER 12

Troxeo actively tried to prevent himself from watching the human leave. He marched swiftly toward his seat at the helm instead. He sat down in the chair and ran a hand through his hair. The things he saw when he entered the bridge bothered him.

The human was standing in the middle of the floor, looking tiny and vulnerable with Arkhan towering over her. Troxeo realized that she must look the same way to others when he spoke to her, but he hadn't thought about it before. The human was getting under his skin, peeling back a layer of his armor every time she looked at him.

"Is something troubling you, cousin?" Arkhan returned to his seat as well. "You don't seem to be yourself."

Troxeo stared out the front window of the ship as he thought about his next moves and even his next sentence. Arkhan didn't realize how correct he was. Troxeo had been second-guessing every thought he'd had in the past several hours.

"Did you get any useful information out of the human during your interrogation?" Troxeo didn't respond. "I know you were in her quarters for some time," Arkhan said innocently.

Troxeo turned to glare at his cousin. He knew what the man implied, and it fueled a fire deep inside him. He didn't know if it was anger or lust, but it burned regardless. "She didn't have much to say."

"Oh, I see. You probably mean there were no words that suited your purpose. Did she speak to you in other ways, perhaps?" Arkhan had an annoying habit of dragging out the end of a sentence to make it have an implied meaning of far more than the literal interpretation of the words themselves.

"What is the matter with you?" Troxeo slammed his fist onto the arm of his chair, feeling it shudder beneath him. "She is an alien from Earth. I didn't fuck her."

Arkhan shrugged. "If you say so. But I would be the last person to criticize you if you decided to pursue it. I mean, she's surprisingly attractive for an Earthling. Somehow I thought they would be repulsive."

Troxeo's throat clenched as he struggled to swallow the first retorts that jumped into his mouth. He couldn't agree out loud with his cousin's appreciation for the human. Nor could he lie openly about his attraction to her. By all rights, the girl should have been nothing more than a piece of luggage. That was what he had intended.

But from the moment she looked into his eyes, there had been a word echoing in the back of his mind. Eleste. It was an ancient word, an old-fashioned idea that most modern Oretoz cast aside as something so silly it might as well be mythical. It was the word used for the deepest connection imaginable between two souls, a link between their bodies, their hearts, and their minds. Troxeo had never known anyone who had experienced such a thing. If they did, they would probably be too embarrassed to talk about it.

He had no connection with Katie's body, not in the obvious sense. Troxeo hadn't experienced sex with the woman. But he swore he could feel her heart beat to the same rhythm as his. And he felt a deeper sense, a primal desire to know more about her and understand her thoughts.

Did that mean she was his eleste? Maybe he was just fascinated by a new, shiny plaything.

"Hello? Troxeo?" Arkhan interrupted his thoughts, and a grin was on his lips. "At any rate, I'm happy to keep the human occupied for you while she's on board the ship. You know, keep an eye on her, make sure she doesn't try to kill herself or find a way to escape, keep her bed warm at night..."

Troxeo was on his feet before he knew it, leaning down over his cousin. "You won't touch her!" He wanted to sink his teeth into Arkhan's throat and rip it out. Every ounce of his body was alive and pulsed with a wild urge that had driven all logic out of him.

Arkhan put his hands up in a placating gesture, but the wicked grin hadn't left his face. "Easy now, Trox. I had no idea you felt so strongly about the cargo. After all, you've been talking about what a disgusting creature she is. I took you at your word."

"She is my prisoner, and she is under my protection." Troxeo's voice sounded rough and gravelly. He tried to look calm, but his muscles were too tense to allow him to sit down again.

On Oretoz, a man and a woman who decided to mate only stayed together for a season. It was enough to ensure there would be a new life to carry on their legacy. A woman was under the protection of her mate while she grew the baby inside her, safe from harm with a strong man at her side during the only time in her life she was vulnerable.

But when a man found his eleste, the connection was different. Instead of being marked as a mate for a few months, the bond was for a lifetime. Something happened during the mating process that changed both of them. Arkhan wondered which sort of protection Troxeo meant.

"Is she now?" Arkhan sat back in his chair, folded his hands against his abdomen, and looked up at his cousin calmly. He had always been content to let others think they were getting the better of him while he gained the upper hand. Troxeo knew this fact about him, but still often found himself trapped. "I wasn't aware that you had taken those steps."

Troxeo groaned. "I meant she is under my protection because I captured her. If you think I am implying anything else, you're delusional."

Arkhan nodded. "That all sounds good, cousin, but there's a problem. What could you do if someone else were to lay his claim on Katie? Then you wouldn't have any control at all." He laughed a little. "I won't pretend to be an expert on humans. My sample size is one. But I find it difficult to believe that she understands how things work for us. How could she know that women have the advantage over the men on Oretoz? They are the ones who decide when it's time to mate and when it's not. I'd be willing to bet I could do what I wanted to with her. I could go into her room, peel back her thin bodysuit, and run my hands over every curve of her little body. She would have no idea that the fact that I'm physically stronger than her doesn't give me all the power in our interaction. If she said no, I would have no choice but to stop."

The image Arkhan projected was something Troxeo had already imagined time after time in his mind. Why was Chixo compelled to give the human an outfit that was barely more than a second skin? It was a darker blue than her haunting eyes, but it only seemed to intensify their color. She had already driven him mad with desire when she wore the clothes from Earth. Seeing her dressed like an Oretoz woman nearly made him tremble inside. It made her look powerful and yet welcoming at the same time.

He longed to do what Arkhan described, to use his power and take what he had desired ever since he took her from the Earth ship. He wanted to feel himself sink into her soft warmth flesh. Troxeo fought to keep his spine straight. If he bent down to get nose-to-nose with his cousin, it would only confirm that Arkhan had succeeded in getting under Troxeo's skin. He was still captain of this ship, and Katie was still his prisoner.

"All I can say, Arkhan, is that you had better keep your hands off her. I am the one who will decide her fate. Not you, not Chixo, and not even Katie herself."

Arkhan calmly got to his feet. He was chest-to-chest with his cousin for only a moment as he pushed past him to the door of the bridge. "Suit yourself, Trox. Just out of curiosity, how long do you think you can protect her once we reach Oretoz? How long do you think it will take the other men to forget she's from Earth and focus on the reality that she isn't as strong as one of our women? We are men who are strengthened by denying ourselves. We are forged by our urges and always in control. It doesn't mean we're perfect."

The door slid shut at Arkhan's back, and Troxeo slumped into his chair once again. Women had never affected him like this before. They had never made him question himself or his morals. It had never bothered him if a woman on Oretoz had been with another man before or after they had spent their time with him. That was how things worked, even if the other man was his cousin.

Katie was different. More than different. Special. He wanted to land on his home planet, dump the rest of his crew, and take the human away to a safe place of their own.

But he was a soldier, and he had orders.

CHAPTER 13

The deep blue orb of Oretoz loomed ahead in the main viewing screen of Troxeo's ship. He had only been away for a short time, but he felt relief wash over him at the idea of returning home. When he was on Oretoz, he knew what his duty was. He didn't have to question his identity, who he was supposed to be, or what he should be feeling. Home was a place where things were straightforward.

On Oretoz, he hoped the last few peculiar days of his life would be over and forgotten, and his regular life would resume. There were no humans here, and his interaction with one particular human would be over.

Troxeo adjusted the ship's computer, shifting the guidance systems to manual control. The ship was capable of landing itself by autopilot, but sometimes he liked to do things the old-fashioned way. He savored the click of the cool buttons under his fingertips and the smooth motion of the acceleration lever as he wrapped his hand around it, pulling it toward himself.

He liked being in control.

The ship quickly burned through the atmospheric barrier, allowing the great city of Metzan to coalesce before him. The capital city of the entire planet, Metzan was a bustling metropolis that seemed to grow every day. Troxeo guided his ship to the Oretoz Capital Fortress in the center of the city. From above it looked enormous, but one could only truly appreciate the unusual size of the building from the ground. Troxeo had stood at the foot of the Fortress many times, staring up at it, soaring into the slate-blue sky, glimmering and slick like glass.

The bottom of the ship gently touched the ground, and Troxeo decelerated the engines, guiding the ship onto its landing pad. He shut down the dashboard with a flick of his finger and turned to Arkhan in the seat next to him. "I'll get the prisoner."

"Are you sure?" his cousin asked. "I'm happy to do it if you like."

"No, thank you." Troxeo bit off his words through tight lips. The mission was his, and he wasn't about to let Arkhan take credit for it by being the person to escort the human into headquarters. Nothing could change whose name was on the mission documentation, but the image of Arkhan leading the first human on Oretoz into the capital would be an effective piece of propaganda.

He left the bridge and followed the looping corridor around to the prisoner's room. When he slid open the door, he found Katie staring out the window, her arms wrapped around herself as she shivered. She looked tiny and frail as she turned to him. "What are you going to do to me now?" she asked in a shaking voice.

Troxeo felt a moment of sympathy for her, but he mentally brushed it aside. He had to remember his responsibilities. "I'm taking you to Commander Reck. Then I will resume my other duties, and my time with you will be over." He grabbed Katie's arm and started to lead her out of the room. His entire hand fit comfortably around her bicep.

"I hope he's nicer than you," she muttered as she tripped over herself on the way to the door.

He smiled down at her. In her eyes, he could see the terror his grin inflicted. "Commander Reck? Nicer than me? You're in for a surprise, Earthling."

Chixo and Arkhan were waiting for him at the bottom of a small ramp that had opened at the back of the ship, allowing them to disembark. His cousin was smiling and looked relaxed, but concern clouded Chixo's face. He didn't bother asking her what her problem was. Troxeo knew it was likely related to the same troubles he was having. It didn't matter, anyway. There was nothing he could do about it.

As they moved toward the large gate leading out of the shipyard with the human stumbling and trembling next to him like a frightened animal, Troxeo noticed a noise he hadn't expected. It was coming from the other side of the high wall that surrounded the ships, and it seemed to grow louder as they approached the gate. He perked up his ears. It wasn't the whine of an engine or the controlled and precise shouts of soldiers drilling. It was cacophonous, a noise built of chaos and perhaps anger.

The gates swung open to reveal more Oretoz than Troxeo had ever seen in one spot before. The crowd even eclipsed the gathering for the election of the current Master Ruler, and that mob of people only got so big because they were commanded to come. The courtyard in front of the building was fenced off, and there were more men on guard duty than normal.

Soldiers formed a double line of security leading away from the gate and toward the Capital Fortress, guarding Katie's path in case someone who had come to see the human managed to slip past the fence with a weapon. Some shouted for her to go back to her planet. Others called for her blood. The people at the edges threatened to push past the lines of military, either because they were angry or because the irritated Oretoz at the back of the crowd mindlessly shoved them forward. Troxeo wrapped his hand around Katie's arm protectively, but he didn't hurry. He couldn't let anyone see he was intimidated.

The small party finally reached another set of gates. These were three times as tall as Troxeo and heavy enough to require five men to pull them open. The howl of the crowd outside subsided as the gates closed behind them. They were now safely in the entryway of the Fortress.

"Troxeo ar Trepniss to see Commander Reck, in the company of Arkhan ar Trepniss, Chixo Velina, and one human."

The guard on duty visibly blanched at the mention of the Earthling, but he quickly recovered with a bow and a murmur. "One moment, sir." He scrambled out of the entryway and disappeared through a small door.

"We seem to be making quite a commotion," Arkhan remarked.

"Shut up."

"Why are there all those people out there?" Katie seemed to get smaller the longer she was on Oretoz. She stared up with giant eyes at everything around her.

When Troxeo didn't answer, Chixo spoke up. "It has to be because of you. They've never seen a human before."

"They don't seem curious. They sounded angry." Katie's voice was nearly a whisper now. "I didn't do anything to them."

The guard reappeared, looking more composed and stopping any of them from replying to the girl. "You should proceed to the personal quarters of Commander Reck."

With a nod, Troxeo and his party headed for one of the elevating pods on the other side of the entryway. Katie was so reticent to move that Troxeo practically had to drag her across the smooth marble floor. After they had entered a pod, they were dumped out onto the one hundred and third floor within moments.

Looking down at Katie, Troxeo stopped before approaching the large silver door that led to the Commander's quarters. "Pull yourself together," he whispered in her ear. "If you think the ride was scary, then you are not going to like Commander Reck at all. Like any of us, he will sense weakness and pounce on it. I suggest you find some strength."

Katie nodded, her eyes looking terrified. For a moment, Troxeo felt protective and wanted to take her fear away. Her chest heaved when she took a deep breath, and he had to look at the floor to avoid distraction. When he glanced back at her, she was standing straighter than before. He only knew she was shaking because he was still holding onto her arm. Troxeo thought it would help her cause to be wearing the bodysuit. Surely even an older warrior like Reck could appreciate her curves.

The silver doors in front of them slid open, and the guards on the other side swiftly parted to make way for the small party. One of them pressed his finger against a keypad, which allowed them into the inner chamber. Commander Reck sat in a throne-like chair behind a desk, not bothering to get up for them as they entered.

Reck had always been old for as long as Troxeo could remember knowing him. He wore a crimson robe over his uniform. It was a symbol of status as well as practical. The Fortress was often chilly. His silver beard looked less majestic than it used to, his jaw line starting to sag. Reck's dark eyes, however, still gazed out from under his hood with the utmost authority. The penetrating stare had helped him rise quickly through the ranks of the military.

"I understand you have completed your mission?" The question seemed redundant as Troxeo led the human up to the edge of the desk. Reck's eyes glittered as he consumed the newcomer with his stare. "Interesting. The humans aren't the same in pictures as they look in real life. It's a bit mesmerizing. I trust that you had no problems retrieving the package?"

"No, sir. The execution was flawless, even if I do say so myself." Troxeo stood at attention, staring out the window behind Reck's shoulder. The city looked gray and blurry below them. He wondered idly if the crowd was still down there, banging on the fences and walls surrounding the Capital Fortress.

"Excellent. Chixo, Arkhan, I thank you for your assistance to Captain Troxeo. It's time for you to return and assume your regular duties now, don't you think?" He didn't look at either of them as he spoke, studying the human instead.

"Sir, if I may speak freely." Chixo took a step forward. "I would like to request that the human be transferred to the research department when you have finished with her. I only had time and equipment to gather initial data on our trip here. I would like to perform several more tests at my leisure and with a full laboratory."

Commander Reck slowly swiveled his head to look at her, his face looking hard. "I know how you like to cut things open, Sergeant Chixo. There may be enough time for you to do everything you want, depending on what happens here. For now, I said to go." He waved her off with a gnarled hand.

"Yes, sir." She and Arkhan left the room without a backward glance.

"Now that we're alone, Troxeo, I have some unusual questions for you. Have you interrogated our prisoner yet?" Reck slowly stood from his chair and came around the desk. He was getting old, but his age had no effect on his stance, and he still had a soldier's bearing. His shoulders looked wide under the black sleeveless shirt, though some of the muscles of his arms had lost their crispness and begun to look soft.

"No, sir." Troxeo was glad that Reck was too focused on the human to catch his lie. His first instinct was to mislead his superior. It hadn't been a successful interrogation, but he had certainly asked Katie questions. Troxeo knew he would be forced to repeat every word to Reck, even some memories he wanted to keep to himself, like how the Earthling had giggled and poked at his muscles.

The older soldier took a position behind the human and examined her from that angle, slowly looking up and down her ass. "That's just as well because I have some very specific information I want to get from her. Do you think she has problems understanding our language?"

"She seems to speak Standard fluently, sir. There have been no communication issues."

Reck's gray eyebrows jumped up like surprised caterpillars as he continued his circle of the human. "That should make my job even easier. For now, I have appointments for the rest of the afternoon. Take the human to holding cell 406. You can return to your regular duties, but keep in mind that I may need your assistance in dealing with the Earthling. Don't go far." He sat down and began examining the paperwork on the desk in front of him as though Troxeo had left already.

"Yes, sir." Troxeo turned from the large desk and pulled the human back out of the Commander's chambers, moving her to a waiting pod. They zoomed to the bottom of the building and went to the underground levels. In the deepest chambers of the building, prisoners were held, guards conducted interrogations, and torturers punished uncooperative soldiers.

His unbidden hopes for the Earthling seemed to plummet along with the descent of the pod. She didn't need to be as far down as cell 406. He knew it was terrible there. In the back of his mind, he had hoped she would be treated as an ambassador of sorts, still held under lock and key but treated respectably. In the farthest reaches of his imagination, he had a secret fantasy that Reck would fire a few questions at her, and everything would be over. He would allow Troxeo to dispose of the human as he liked. Troxeo would gladly whisk her back to his quarters and finally do what he had dreamed of since he locked eyes with her on the Earthling ship.

For the time being, Katie's future was in room 406.

CHAPTER 14

From the moment they landed on Oretoz, Katie had problems getting her legs to move. They seemed to have turned to liquid and become useless, along with her stomach. Troxeo had told her to be strong when they went in to see Commander Reck, and she had done her best. Katie could only remain standing because she wasn't required to speak to him. Either she had done a decent job of being brave, or the older alien had been too busy to notice how badly her knees were shaking.

Any trace of bravery that she did have disappeared as Troxeo took her down to her cell. She had nearly begun to think of him as being on her side as he guarded her against the roaring crowds in the city and supported her outside of Commander Reck's office. But she realized now that she couldn't have any allies here. Not Arkhan, not Chixo, and certainly not Troxeo. He had been the one to take her in the first place, after all. She was doomed.

The violent motion of the pod made what was left of her stomach shoot up and out of her mouth during their descent. It was very similar to the elevators she knew back home, only smaller and rounder; she and the aliens had to squeeze tightly together if they all wanted to fit in the same one. Most things on Oretoz so far seemed to be like the pods: similar but not the same. The sky was blue, but it was more of a slate blue than the sky on Earth. It made the colors of the buildings and plants stand out more, like the brilliant hues that stood out just after a thunderstorm had cleared.

She had seen a good sampling of the people as they screamed at her and pounded against the fence, and they seemed to be much like Earthlings in that they had a variety of hair, eye, and skin colors. They were all slightly different shapes. The one thing they had in common that wasn't similar to the humans she knew was that they all had perfect bodies. Every single one of the people in the crowd, either man or woman, was positively ripped with muscles. Katie doubted they knew anything about fast food, frozen dinners, or curling up on the couch in front of the television.

The pod stopped, and Troxeo guided her off it with a firm grip on her upper arm. She was certain she would have his fingers permanently imprinted on her skin by the time they finished. The new floor was crisp and bright. The floors and walls seemed to be made from something like sealed concrete, hard and glossy, but without any visible seams. The beams that came down from the ceiling were so bright that she couldn't see any light fixtures.

The two guards waiting for them on the other side of the pod doors joined them as Troxeo guided her across the smooth floor. Katie's feet were ready to give up and drag behind her as the big man led her to her doom. But she forced herself to continue moving one foot in front of the other. The Oretoz thought she was weak, and she didn't want to prove them right. Katie felt like she was representing humanity.

When they stopped, the sign in front of her must have said 406 in the native language. She couldn't read the gibberish printed on it. The sign hung on a rectangular cage in the middle of the room. The bars were white and narrowly spaced. There were even bars across the top even though she knew there would never be any hope of climbing out that way. It reminded Katie of a giant hamster cage, and she was the hamster. Troxeo led her in through the door.

"She has to be stripped, Captain," one of the guards said. He licked his lips, and Troxeo jumped slightly.

Katie looked up at him, and her gaze locked onto his green eyes. There was something in there, a spark of emotion. She thought it was something more than a soldier doing his job. She had tried several times to write him off as an enemy, but she always changed her mind when she looked at him. Katie knew he was her captor, but she suspected that deep down there was more to him than what he showed on the surface.

Apparently he wasn't going to let his depths show now. With his mouth set in a grim line, he stuck his fingers into the collar of her bodysuit. They were warm and hard as they touched her collar bone. He yanked down swiftly and split the suit in half, the slippery pieces of blue material falling away from her body. She wrapped her arms around herself, but it was no use. There was no place to hide in the cage, and she couldn't possibly cover all the parts of her that she didn't want anyone to see.

"Please," she whimpered, looking up at her captor with uncertainty. "Please don't do this to me, Troxeo."

He said nothing. He dropped the scraps of fabric that remained in his fist and let them fall to the floor. The big man hesitated for a fraction of a second, just long enough to make her wonder what he was going to do next. His gaze lingered over her naked body, and she felt even more exposed than before. His green eyes burned with a fire behind them. She cringed, waiting for him to scoop her up and ravage her.

But he kept himself under control, turning and stepping out through the door of the cage. He never stopped and didn't look back, marching on until she couldn't see him anymore.

Katie fell to the floor of the cage in exhaustion. The skin on her back stung from the hard surface. One of the guards shut and locked the door before marching away. Katie looked around, searching for any hope of rescue or escape. But the only things she could see were more cages. They were spread throughout the enormous room, twenty feet away from each other, stretching off into the distance. The cages closest to her were unoccupied, but she could see the shapes of other nude forms further away. Were they from Oretoz or were they other strangers taken from their far-away homes?

Her vision blurred as tears pooled up in her eyes and fell onto her cheeks. She was being held captive on an alien planet, and there was nothing she could do about it.

* * *

Someone slid a meal through a tiny opening in the bars near the floor. Katie's stomach rumbled, but she considered ignoring the food. Perhaps it would be easier to starve to death and choose her fate herself. But she ate despite her reservations, gambling that she still had a faint hope of escape.

The guards had presented her with a platter that wasn't nearly as appealing as the food Troxeo had brought her on the ship. The round balls of bread were hard and stale, the fruit had gone mushy, and the slab of meat had an odd sheen to it that made her stomach wretch. She assumed the drink was water, but it tasted bitter and stale.

The guards brought her a bucket shortly after they took away her food tray. She knew its purpose even before the stench of it hit her nostrils. It was embarrassing enough to be naked, but now she had to pee out in the open, in front of everyone? She was spared further embarrassment when the guards left her to her own devices, marching off to bring trays or offer buckets to more distant prisoners.

The door to her cage swung open. She didn't know how long she had been waiting. There were no windows down here, and she hadn't had a sense of time since she left Earth. There were no sunrises or sunsets to measure the passing hours, but she felt as though she had been lying on the hard floor for days.

"I suggest you get up," said a voice above her.

Katie cracked open a dry eyelid to see the stout form of Commander Reck. He loomed over her, fists on his hips and wooly eyebrows pressed together in consternation. She didn't have the energy to be afraid of him any longer. She pulled herself to a sitting position and gestured at the floor in front of her. "Please, make yourself comfortable.

It's so sweet of you to visit. Would you like something to drink?"

Katie wasted her sarcasm. "I'll stand," Reck said as he sneered at her. "I've come to ask you a few questions. First of all, what do you know about Earth's plans for invading other planets?"

She looked up at him with bleary eyes. "I work for a finance company. I used to, at least. If you'd like to ask me about their interest rates on personal loans, I'd be happy to help you learn all about it. But I don't work for the government or the military. No one has invited me to sit in on any of the EarthGov assemblies, so I don't know anything about plans for invasion. Maybe we will and maybe we won't. Either way, I never thought it would affect me until Troxeo took me from my ship."

Reck stroked his chin with his thumb and forefinger and paced around the cage. Fortunately, the smelly bucket had been removed at some point by a guard whose job Katie didn't envy. "Tell me about your general knowledge, then. What does Earth know about Oretoz?"

Katie sighed. They were only on the second question, and the interrogation was already getting old. "Nothing, as far as I know. I had never heard of the place until Troxeo mentioned it."

"Really?" he fired back. "You were on your way to Bonaan, so apparently humans have perfected interstellar travel."

"Discovering Bonaan was an accident. There are plenty of planets with life in the universe. Do you think you're a special snowflake? No one on Earth knows about you, and even if they did, they probably wouldn't care." *And nobody knows I'm here*, she thought. Maybe starving to death was a better idea than she realized.

"What about your weapons technology? What arms do you have prepared in the event of intergalactic war?" Commander Reck was standing across the cage from her with his hands behind his back.

"Intergalactic war?" Katie thought she might be able to pinch herself and wake up at a science fiction convention. "I don't know. I keep telling you, I don't know anything about this stuff. If you wanted someone who knows things, you should have told Troxeo to grab a military strategist and leave me the hell alone."

Reck's brows drew closer together, his dark eyes intense beneath them. "I have ways of making you talk, and they are ways I am not ashamed to use. A few rounds of electricity might spark your memory."

"Do me a favor and make sure you crank it all the way up to the setting where it fries me, okay?" Katie smirked in spite of herself. She would never have spoken to someone like that before. Apparently being in space had changed her. That or the knowledge that she would die soon no matter what happened here.

"Your insolence and hostility will get you nowhere, Earthling." He stood over her, looking menacing.

"Yeah, because cooperation has gotten me into the penthouse of the Hilton," she muttered. "I'm just an average person who gets up and goes to work every morning. I lead a very boring life. I can't tell you what I don't know. Do you want me to start making stuff up?"

Reck considered her for a moment before speaking. "We have found that people often know more than they realize. We have mind control specialists that are highly trained in retrieving such information. Unfortunately, it is a risky process for the patient. Sometimes the rest of the mind is left completely useless." Katie had a horrified look on her face.

"If I allow you to take a tour of this floor, you will have the opportunity to see several victims of this process. They can't speak or hear at all any longer. They shit where they sleep. They are mere shells of their former selves." He took a step closer to her. All she could see as she looked up at him was the paunch of his belly and his cruel face. "I hear it's quite painful."

Katie wasn't sure anything compared to the pain of being ripped away from her homeland. But she wasn't going to tell Reck that.

"I'll be back tomorrow," the commander continued, "and I expect you to have come up with better answers." A guard swung open the cage door for him. He moved swiftly through and marched off into the distance.

Katie lay on the floor and closed her eyes, tears dripping silently from her face. For the first time since she had boarded the spaceship to Bonaan, she thought about

Ben. It was his cheating ass that had inspired her to leave Earth in the first place. If she ever made it back home, she was going to kick him straight in the balls. Then she thought about her mother, whose face had looked concerned as they said their goodbyes at the spaceport. Katie hoped she would have the chance someday to tell her she was right. Her thoughts strayed to strange flashes of her past and her possible future as she fell asleep.

When she awoke, another familiar face stared down at her from the other side of the bars. It was small and pointy, with pale skin and a mane of spiked hair that stood out around it. Katie was looking from nearly the same vantage point she had seen Chixo before, only at that time no bars had been between them.

The alien woman shook her head. "You and those giant breasts of yours. I still say you ought to let me get them fixed for you."

"No, thank you." Katie rolled over and crossed her arms over her ample chest. The floor of her cell was cold as well as hard, and her joints and limbs were stiff from sleeping on it.

"Oh, come on. Don't be like that. I have something to tell you."

Katie rolled over to glare at Chixo, but she didn't remove her arms from her breasts. "What do you want?"

"I have a message for you from Arkhan." Chixo licked her lips, looking for the right words to say. "He's trying to get you out of here. He's on guard duty for this building tomorrow, and he thinks he can pull it off." Her words were barely above a whisper, but she had every ounce of Katie's attention.

"But why?" Katie knew she should be grateful and going along with the flow instead of asking questions, but she couldn't help herself. Chixo's actions seemed odd. Katie sat up and moved closer to the woman. "Why would anyone rescue me now?"

Chixo shook her spiky head. "He said something about being under the impression that you were going to be an ambassador instead of a prisoner. And apparently Reck mentioned killing you if he isn't satisfied with your interrogation tomorrow."

"What about Troxeo?" Katie demanded. "Will he help me, too?"

Chixo gave a snort of laughter. "That one? No way. He's into following the rules. He'd never do anything the commander told him not to do."

Katie felt her heart sink. Each of the cousins was terrifying in their own way, but she had hoped Troxeo would be the one to save her. He seemed more confident, more knowledgeable, and more likely to pull it off. She knew from experience how strong he was. "Oh. I was hoping...I don't know what I was hoping."

Chixo scanned the large room for guards. "Here's the deal. I have a write-up authorizing Arkhan and me to take you to the research department for deeper scans. It's a forgery, so I don't know how far we'll get with it.

But the research department isn't housed in this building. It's a good excuse to get you out of here. I don't think anyone will question us until we're headed out to the shipyard. If we make it that far, we can probably run for our ship if we get caught. Enan will have the ship warmed up and ready to go. All you have to do is cooperate with us when we come to get you."

It was strange to hear the outline of a devious plan from someone who seemed cold and scientific, but maybe Chixo was exactly the sort of person required for an escape like this. It was nice to hear Enan was involved. The engineer was strange, but he seemed like he had a good heart. He was a lot like most of the geeks she knew back on Earth. "Okay. I don't have a lot of options. I'll do whatever you tell me to do."

"I'm serious about this," Chixo warned. "Depending on who we run into and where we go, I may need you to act perfectly normal, or to pass out, or run like crazy, and I'll need your immediate cooperation. You're going to have to trust me. I know you aren't a trained soldier, but you need to act like one."

Katie nodded. "I'll do my best."

Chixo's eyes swept over her nude body. "I have an energy capsule to give you, but you don't have any place to conceal it right now. I'll bring it to you when I come back. You'll have to bite down on it right away."

"I will do whatever I need to do. Thank you."

The alien shook her head. "I wouldn't thank me until we're safely out of here. We might never escape. I'll see you tomorrow morning." With a glance in both directions, Chixo turned and disappeared.

CHAPTER 15

Commander Reck was drumming his fingers impatiently on his desk when Troxeo arrived. He was never a particularly pleasant person to look at since he was always scowling, but Troxeo could tell immediately that the older man wasn't happy.

"Did you want to see me, sir?"

"No, I don't want to," the commander snapped, "but it seems I have to since the human you brought back is worthless." He slapped a hand on the surface of his desk.

"Pardon me for asking, sir, but how? She seemed fine when I left her in her cell." His stomach dropped at the idea that something might have happened to her. What could it have been? An overzealous guard? An Oretoz disease fatal to humans?

"The creature's physical health is of no concern to me as long as she can answer my questions, but she doesn't appear to want to cooperate." He leaned forward on the desk. Reck steepled his fingers together and had a grim look on his face. "The Earthling, Troxeo, is useless to me. It's the textbook definition of a failed mission."

Troxeo felt several beads of sweat pop out on his forehead. He knew Reck could leave a terrible mark on his record. "With all due respect, sir, I brought you a human. You specified no other qualifications. If I remember correctly, you said you didn't want a scientist or anyone high up in their chain of command."

Reck's left eye twitched in irritation. "I'm not in the mood to play games with the precise wording of your assignment. If you're correct, then I changed my mind. This Earthling doesn't know anything. I had imagined that the average human would have a general working knowledge of affairs on Earth, but this one pretends it knows nothing. Either it's truly as stupid as it looks or it's more stubborn than you are."

Troxeo didn't reply. He couldn't; he didn't know what to say. His orders were to bring back an average human, and he had certainly done that. Commander Reck was known for his unexpected moves and decisions. It made him a terrifying foe to face in a battle, and unfortunately a demanding superior officer as well.

He couldn't tell if Katie was playing stupid or telling the truth. All her answers to his questions came under the influence of the epobaka juice. What she knew wasn't as important as the information Reck desired.

The older soldier sighed and ran a hand through his shock of gray hair. "Look, Captain, I have my superiors breathing down my neck and demanding answers. We need to know if it's worth it to invade Earth. The working theory from our strategists is that we can reap the natural resources available, and the humans won't be smart enough or powerful enough to fight back effectively. I'm going to interview the prisoner again tomorrow, and I need results this time. You're going to get them for me."

"How do you expect me to do that, sir?" Troxeo asked, trying not to sound too impertinent. He could suggest they use the bright blue extract again, but he didn't want Katie to mention that Troxeo had already administered a dose to her. Unauthorized use of a truth serum on an interplanetary prisoner would go on his record right alongside the large red 'Failed Mission' stamp that hovered above it in his mind.

"Bring your weapons. You're going to help me coax the information out of the creature, slowly and painfully. If it still doesn't cooperate, then you will dispose of it."

"Dispose of it, sir?" Was this what he had been waiting for? Could he brandish a knife at the woman for a little bit until Reck was tired of playing with her? When the show was over, he could throw her on his shoulder and take her home. His heart thudded a little at the hope, and one of his other organs responded as well.

"Yes, kill it." Reck looked at Troxeo as though he had suddenly gone soft, and Troxeo thought he might be right. "I'm not going to spend the money to feed and guard the thing if it's no use to me. But when it's gone, I can send you back to get another one. Perhaps you'll be able to find one that has more qualifications than a smart mouth."

Troxeo gave a stiff nod. Kill the human? He searched for a way around the order, but he knew there was no escape. The commander would want to see the job done in front of him; he always enjoyed the spurt of fresh blood. There was no chance of starting a ruse. He wouldn't have the opportunity to take her outside the prison, then steal her away.

He couldn't refuse the order, either. The human was part of his mission, and he was responsible for her. If Reck told him to kill her, he would have to obey.

Commander Reck dismissed him with a flick of his hand.

That night, Troxeo sat in his quarters and sharpened his knives. He ran the sharpening stone carefully down the blades, honing them to the finest point he could manage. If he was required to do a horrible job, then he was going to do it correctly. If he refused, he could be demoted, shunned, or worse. What sort of future awaited if the army expelled him? A terrible one.

With every ring of the stone against metal, he loathed himself a little bit more.

What was happening to him? Just a few days ago, he had been a high-ranking officer with a perfect record. He had never faltered in the directives given by his commander, willing slaughtering or capturing the enemy with impunity. He'd never felt guilty about anything he had done before. There was no reason to as long as he was living the glorified life of a soldier.

But Katie was changing him. He could have done anything he liked to her on the way back to Oretoz. His commander wouldn't have complained if he had pinned her to the bunk and buried himself deep inside her. His groin warmed at the thought. She could have fought and screamed, and nobody would have come to her rescue. She was his captive, not a high-born female warrior of Oretoz. He had every right to take advantage of her, and he certainly wanted to.

Why didn't he?

Arkhan would have slapped him on the shoulder and asked for a turn. Even Chixo, with her slightly softer sentiments, wouldn't have objected. If anything, she would have asked to watch.

Katie had looked up at him with her big blue eyes under a fringe of dark hair, breasts heaving in fear, and he couldn't bring himself to do it. He pushed away the word that kept dancing at the back of his head: eleste. But a human couldn't be his soulmate. While his fellow soldiers would have applauded him for raping a captive, they would not approve of a love match with an Earthling.

And when he had put her in that cage...He set his knives down, no longer able to concentrate on the sharpening process. Troxeo knew prisoners were stripped naked, and their captors had the right to do it themselves if they so chose. But he had hoped he wouldn't have to be the one to do it to Katie. He wanted to turn on his heel and put the whole fiasco behind him, but the guard had insisted Troxeo assert his privilege and do it himself.

When he had wrapped his fingers in the collar of her bodysuit, he felt her warmth and fear. He was caught between her wishes and his reputation. With the guards looking at him, reputation had won. Even though he regretted his actions, he did not regret the results.

The bodysuit had fluttered to the floor, revealing the ripe deliciousness of Katie's body. The Oretoz clothing had been flattering, but it was nothing compared to the glory underneath it. Her voluptuous breasts tapered to a tiny waist that expanded back out to her hips, hips which were the perfect size to wrap his hands around. It was hard not to stare, and even harder not to pin her to the floor of the cage and take her immediately. Again, the guards would not have minded. It was his right and his privilege, and they were probably down there right now wondering why he didn't take advantage.

He rolled into his bunk and tried to get his mind focused on other things. He would never be able to sleep now. When he closed his eyes, he could see nothing but her naked, quaking body in front of him. His hard cock plagued him, yet he had no outlet for it. Troxeo supposed he could visit one of the clubs and find a woman interested in mating. It would take care of him physically, but it wasn't what he needed. He longed for something more than fucking. He wanted a deeper connection, and he knew he would soon be ordered to kill the woman with whom he wanted to connect.

CHAPTER 16

Katie hadn't slept. Her mind was active and running at full speed, imagining all the possibilities Chixo and Arkhan might have for her rescue. She had seen little of the building she was currently in, and she knew nothing about its management. She couldn't possibly be any help in planning, and yet she began taking note of the guards, trying to measure the time between their patrols and listening to what they said.

In the end, she had nothing helpful to contribute.

She worried they wouldn't come. Just because Chixo said they were going to rescue her didn't mean it would happen. They didn't owe her anything. What if their plans were spoiled before they made it to Katie's cell? What if someone realized the signed authorization to take Katie to the research department wasn't real, and Chixo was imprisoned in a distant cage of her own? What if their plan was only partially successful and Katie ended up in the research department?

She shuddered at the thought of the poking and prodding she was likely to get there. She clearly remembered Chixo mentioning something about a captive breeding program for humans. She imagined a room made of glass walls, where she would be forced to have sex with strangers while the aliens watched and took notes.

Katie's wandering thoughts were soon interrupted by the sound of approaching footsteps. Katie twisted around to see both Arkhan and Chixo speak to one of the guards and show him a fake document. The guard let them pass with a nod before continuing on his patrol.

Chixo opened the door to the cage and tossed a new bodysuit at Katie. This one was dark gray. "Put this on."

Arkhan hovered at her shoulder, a leering grin on her face as he unashamedly took in Katie's body. "I don't know. We could leave her as she is. I rather like her this way."

"Shut up and keep watch for the guards. We don't have a lot of time." She stepped toward Katie, who was zipping up the bodysuit, and shoved a capsule in her mouth. "Bite down on this."

Feeling like a dog who had been force-fed a pill, Katie clenched her jaw and glared angrily in Chixo's direction. "You could have handed it to me." The capsule released a tart liquid into her mouth, and she felt her body become tense and ready for action.

The alien woman gave her an impatient look. "Can we stop arguing about things and start moving?" She ushered Katie out of the cage.

"Don't forget these. Hold your hands out." Arkhan clamped a slim band of metal around each of her wrists and pushed a small button on the side of one of them. The bands immediately stuck to each other, pinning her hands in front of her.

No matter how hard she pulled, Katie couldn't get them apart. "What the hell are these? And why am I wearing them? I wasn't in handcuffs when we came in here."

The alien winked at her. "Don't bother trying to get them off. They're electromagnetic. We would look a lot more suspicious if you walked alongside us without any restraints. Nobody would willingly go to the research department. No offense, Chixo."

She snorted. "Whatever. Let's go."

With Chixo holding one of her arms and Arkhan holding the other, the three of them moved through the large prison floor, passing numerous cages on the way. Only a few had people in them. Instead of looking at them, Katie stared at the ground moving under her feet. She reminded herself that there was nothing she could do to save them, but it didn't make her feel any better.

Chixo whispered in her ear when there wasn't anyone around. "Listen to me. Don't talk to anyone, no matter how you feel. You're a prisoner, and you need to act like one. Keep your head down and do what we say."

Katie merely nodded. She wasn't sure if she could reply even if she wanted to. Her mouth and throat felt as though cotton had swabbed them.

Nobody questioned Katie when they reached the elevator pods. She assumed Chixo had already taken care of any necessary paperwork. Their pod swooped upwards, Katie's stomach plummeting to her feet as they rose. When they emerged on the ground floor, Chixo flashed a document at the guards stationed on either side of the door. They barely glanced at it before waving the three of them through.

Emerging from the fortress, Katie couldn't help but look up and around. She'd had a brief glance at Oretoz on her way in, but it wasn't enough for her to be satisfied. They stepped into a courtyard paved with beautiful green stones that glimmered in the sunlight.

A strong, tall fence surrounded the yard. It was the one the Oretoz populace had pummeled against as Troxeo had led her inside. Katie had been expecting a sophisticated barrier developed from alien technology. By all appearances, it was no different than a regular iron fence she would find back on Earth. It stood out against the slate-blue sky, emerald trees in the distance breaking up the horizon with curving limbs. The crowd of people was gone. No one expected the Earth girl to leave the fortress right now.

"The building to our left houses the research department," Chixo whispered.

Katie cocked her head to look at it. It was squat and square, like a giant cube. Similar to the building they had just left, it appeared to be made of a substance smoother than glass, and it shone in the brilliant light.

"Put your head down!" Chixo admonished. "You're a prisoner, not a tourist, remember?"

Katie immediately lowered her gaze to the ground again.

"Which one is Enan on?" the alien woman asked over Katie's head.

"I wanted something small," Arkhan replied. "A ship that will blend into the background. He should have one of the land hoppers ready for us to use."

"Just a land hopper? That's not going to get us very far." For the first time, Chixo looked doubtful.

"Well, what did you think we were going to do? Fly out of here on one of the intergalactic ships and wave goodbye to the commander as we warp out of here? It's obvious, and security will be too tight. We can't help leaving a trail. Let's make it a small one."

Arkhan's grip tightened on Katie's arm as they headed to the shipyard. "Ow, that hurts!" she exclaimed. "You're supposed to treat me better than in prison, right?"

The big man didn't apologize. In fact, he closed his hand more firmly around her arm and walked faster toward their awaiting ride.

Katie hadn't had a chance to get a good look at the shipyard when they had first landed. She was too stunned and disoriented to take in the giant gleaming birds that filled it. There were ships of every shape and size, every one of them polished and bright. Tiny pods with fans of blades over them resembled miniature helicopters. Gigantic ships that could have swallowed a 747 for breakfast were further down the yard, with massive engines designed for intergalactic travel. She recognized the ship on which she had arrived. It had an odd round shape that reminded her of a slightly squashed beet.

The aliens guided her toward one of the small vessels. She could see Enan through the front window, tightly wedged into a confined space. On the side of the ship, a door was open with a ladder descending from it. Arkhan shoved her up and into the vehicle. The climb was short but difficult because she didn't have full use of her hands. Chixo followed behind her. The inside of the plane was a little cramped, but Katie wasn't going to complain. The rear of the land hopper had several seats and Katie tentatively chose one.

Chixo called out to Arkhan. "Where are you going? The ship's right here!"

Katie peered out one of the round windows. The big man trotted across the shipyard to one of the beet-shaped ships. He crawled underneath it, and his arm muscles rippled as he pulled at something. Within a minute, he emerged with a handful of electronics and was coming back to their ship and up the ladder.

"What was that all about?" Chixo demanded.

"I was making sure no one's following us," Arkhan replied with a grin. "I yanked the starting mechanism out of Troxeo's ship."

Katie felt her stomach turn inside-out at the mention of the man's name. Troxeo terrified and intrigued her, and she was surprised to experience a feeling of disappointment. Was Troxeo her enemy? Of course, he had been the one to strip her of her clothes back in the cage. She couldn't let herself forget that.

"He wouldn't try to stop us, would he?" she asked.

Arkhan barked out a laugh as he slammed the door. "My cousin is predictable. He is an agent of Commander Reck, and he'll never be anything else. Don't think for a second that he has any pity for you. I have no doubt that he would do everything in his power to stop us." He took his place in a seat next to Enan and began pushing buttons.

The ship glided out of its slot and lifted off into the air. Katie turned and pressed her face to the window behind her, looking toward the fortress. There didn't seem to be any frantic guards chasing after them or pointing guns in their direction. In fact, the whole place looked quiet and peaceful from the outside. She sat back in her seat and relaxed against the smooth upholstery.

Katie had a long way to go before she was home, but she was on her way.

CHAPTER 17

The life of a soldier usually provided excellent sleep. After a typical day of vigorous training and plenty of mental exercise, Troxeo was ready to crash into his bunk. He rarely dreamed, but when he did, he forgot his dreams by morning.

Last night had been different. From the moment he closed his eyes, he dreamed of nothing but the human. He relived his conquest of the Earth spaceship when he first saw her, only this time he didn't sling her over his shoulder. He scooped her into his arms and looked down into her eyes. In his dream, it wasn't a kidnapping. She wanted to go with him. She wanted to be with him.

He saw himself with her in the prison cell again. There were no guards this time, and it was Katie herself who demanded that he strip her. He could feel the smooth material of her bodysuit ripping, revealing the pearlescent wonder of her body. She wrapped her strong legs around him and pressed her lips to his. When he awoke, the warmth of her body dissipated with the night.

His dreams haunted him as he made himself ready for the interrogation. Troxeo knew his day would not be a sexual adventure. He would be forced to watch someone torture Katie. He might even be the one doing it. He couldn't stand the thought of his blade piercing her smooth skin, not when he could be running his hands over it lovingly instead. No method was below Commander Reck's standards.

As Troxeo showered, he wondered if Reck was as attracted to the girl as he was. If the old man laid a hand on her, Troxeo might do something that would get him executed. There was no way to know the truth until it happened. He dressed and ate with efficiency, but without excitement. He knew he would regret this day for the rest of his life.

The fortress was quiet this morning. They were supposed to arrive at the prisoner's cell early, before breakfast. Troxeo thought about Katie as he marched through the empty hallways, concerned for her comfort as well as her safety. When had he become so soft that he was worried about whether or not a prisoner was hungry? He would have to make sure he didn't say anything about the conditions in which the human was living. No honorable soldier would notice them, much less care what happened to an off-worlder.

He arrived at Commander Reck's office precisely on time. He wouldn't dare to be late and never liked arriving early. Reck was pacing back and forth, recording a video on the computer. "There will be substantial repercussions if my orders are not carried forth to the letter. I trust that you already know this, but given recent events, I feel the need to repeat it. Don't start thinking on your own, and don't disappoint me." He turned to look at Troxeo. "I hope that you're feeling as good about today as I am."

"I am confident our mission will be successful, sir." He had said the same words many times before at the beginning of missions or battles, but he had never realized how stiff and robotic they sounded until now.

“You can give me all the prattle you want, Captain, but I’ve come up with a few ideas.” The older man turned to the window and stroked his short beard. “I haven’t changed my basic plan, mind you. If the Earthling still refuses to talk at the end of the day, I want it dead. I don’t like the idea of a foreign creature being in my fortress to begin with, much less the notion of it escaping and ruining things.”

That must be exactly how I sounded, thought Troxeo. I thought of Katie as nothing more than an animal, barely worthy of her gender and incapable of anything but grunting and shitting. He recoiled inside at the idea that a living being as beautiful and intelligent as Katie was being treated this way.

Commander Reck interrupted his revolutionary thoughts. “I’ve decided to try a different tactic first. The human didn’t seem to care too much when I threatened it with pain or the mind-control specialists. Do you think it understood what those things were? Even if it doesn’t, I’m sure it will understand the idea of going home.”

“You’re going to send her home?” He became excited for a fraction of a second at the thought of being the person to bring her back to Earth and seeing her face light up when she saw her home planet again. She would feel grateful toward him, wouldn’t she?

"Haven't you been listening, Captain?" Reck demanded. "I just said I still wanted it dead. But that doesn't mean I can't manipulate the human before I kill her. First, I will imply I may send it home if it cooperates. If the human is willing to answer my questions thoroughly, and not just give me some shit about not knowing again, I'll promise it a free ride home. I'm smart enough to know that some creatures will respond better to a bribe than to a threat. Of course, its carcass will never make it out of the prison."

Troxeo swallowed. Reck's words had shattered his last hope. "As you wish, sir."

"Let's get on with it, shall we?" Reck led the way out of his chambers, down the elevating pods, and into the prison.

As they wound their way through the numerous cages, Troxeo's heart and stomach competed for space in his throat. He would make sure he didn't look the Earthling in the eyes, but it would be impossible to tune out her angelic voice. There was nothing he could do to prepare for the task ahead of him.

When they reached cell number 406, it was empty.

CHAPTER 18

Troxeo had his gun at the ready as he approached the Earthling's cell. He knew Katie would be furious if nothing else. Even though she was no threat to him or anyone else with training as an Oretoz soldier, he couldn't go into her cell acting like he trusted her. It would reveal all the feelings he had been working to eliminate.

In the end, his armaments were irrelevant. It hadn't mattered that he had fully charged his blaster and sharpened his knives. There wasn't a prisoner on whom to use them.

Commander Reck stood at his shoulder, taking in the scene before him. Troxeo knew his superior officer saw the same thing he did. The floor of the cage was empty. The door was closed and locked. It made it look like Katie had slipped through the bars or melted through the floor, behaving like an ethereal being they couldn't hope to understand or catch.

Troxeo had an odd feeling in the pit of his stomach, an automatic alarm that immediately made him think of his cousin. Arkhan helped him capture the prisoner, but would he have worked on his own to free her?

"Where is the human? Guard!" Commander Reck barked, his deep voice echoing in the large room. His jowls wavered with every word. "The prisoner was supposed to be here, but this cell is empty. Who was on watch?"

A young guard came running over from his station by the elevator pod doors. "I don't know, sir. I only started my shift a few minutes ago." He quickly pulled up the prison records on a computer, fingers flying over the screen. "Apparently the Earthling has been taken to the Research Department."

"When did the transfer occur?" Reck's voice sounded ominous.

The young guard consulted the computer again. "It was this morning, sir, during the shift change."

"I'm going to have a long discussion with whoever authorized the move. Who signed off on the transfer?" the older man raged.

Drops of sweat were visible on the young guard's forehead. He gulped a few times, his breath becoming labored when he discovered the answer to the commander's question. "It looks like you did, sir." He looked up at the older man, eyes wide with fear.

As Commander Reck's face slowly turned purple from the neck up, Troxeo felt a little sorry for the young guard. What was the guard supposed to do if the computer told him Katie went to the Research Department under Reck's authority? He was only relaying the information. Troxeo was sure Chixo had forged the records. He shook his head. The girl was an expert at hacking into computer systems. She had done it numerous times when they were children, just to see how far she could go. Unfortunately, the fact that the fake document said they had permission to take the prisoner to the Research Department was like an arrow pointing directly to her.

Troxeo fully expected the commander to exact a demeaning punishment on the guard. Anyone who accused Reck of doing something foolish disappeared for a while. But instead of ordering the guard to the electrocution room, Reck gave him a different order. "Try to get a hold of someone in Research. Confirm they received the prisoner." He paced back and forth as he waited, heavy boots beating out a staccato rhythm on the hard floor.

The guard touched a button on the earpiece of his communicator. "This is Private 126 in the Fortress. I need to speak with the receiving guard in the Research Department." He waited for a moment while he was connected. "I would like to confirm the transfer of the human prisoner to your building." He listened, and his skin paled visibly. "I see. Thank you. Signing off." He touched the button on his earpiece again. The young guard swallowed, and Troxeo didn't need to hear him speak. He knew the news wasn't good. "There's nothing in our records to indicate anyone received the prisoner, sir."

"Of course not!" Reck roared. "I should have known the idea of bringing a human to Oretoz would never work. Reck pointed at the guard. "You come with me to the Research Department. I want to confirm that the prisoner is gone, and her disappearance is not a system malfunction. No good will come from sounding an alarm if the human is still safely within the walls of the Fortress. I also want to see who had the balls to sign my name on fake orders. He pointed a thick finger at Troxeo. "Head outside and search the grounds. If the timestamp on the transfer requisition is correct, the human can't have gone far."

Troxeo nodded, surprised that Commander Reck was operating in a relatively level-headed manner. He had seen the older man slaughter most of the soldiers around him after a failed maneuver or a training session that was going badly. Troxeo was privately glad they were taking precautions before announcing the escape. It would give him more time to find Katie before anyone else did.

He trotted to one of the elevator pods and jumped inside. Troxeo tapped his fingers impatiently against the circular wall as he rode up. There was no way Katie could have escaped without help. Getting out of the Fortress alive would require a native's knowledge of the system, the people, and the rules. Katie's only weapon was sass. That wouldn't get her far with any Oretoz, who understood strength and weapons better than wordplay.

Someone helped Katie escape. She must have had an accomplice or two, and Arkhan and Chixo were the most likely suspects. They knew her. Chixo probably felt sorry for the girl, and Troxeo was sure she would have loved to see the inside of a functioning human body if the opportunity presented itself. Arkhan, on the other hand, was only participating for himself. He had told Troxeo in no uncertain terms about his interest in the Earthling.

When his pod arrived at the ground floor, Troxeo headed swiftly for the front door. The guard was practically asleep until he noticed Troxeo striding across the foyer with determination. At that point, he snapped to attention and muttered something deferential. Troxeo ignored him. He had no time for pleasantries, even if they were proper military protocol.

He burst into the courtyard, scanned the green stones that paved the ground and the tall fence surrounding the area. The place was practically empty. Troxeo headed for a gate that would take him to the surrounding city, but the sound of a ship's engines made him look up. A small land hopper rose up out of the shipyard, leaving a trail of white exhaust against the dark blue sky. It hovered overhead for a moment, then zipped off to the east.

Troxeo's heart sank. Before any ship took off on an authorized flight, a warning alarm sounded throughout the courtyard. The conspicuous absence of any noise meant the hopper's movement was unsanctioned.

He raced across the courtyard toward the gates that led to the holding area for all the ships. Troxeo hadn't bothered to grab a communicator on his way out of the Fortress, and he wasn't about to go back and get one now. He had to catch up with that hopper.

Once Troxeo made it past the gate, he started moving for his ship. It was larger and slower than the land hopper, but he would have to make it work. It would take too long to obtain access to a smaller vessel, and he wanted to get into the air before the rogue ship had a chance to get too far out of range. He clambered up the ramp, slammed himself into the pilot's seat, pushed his left hand against the fingerprint panel and punched the ignition with his right hand.

Nothing happened.

Troxeo was waiting for the ship's instruments to light up and the engine to start rumbling underneath him, but he didn't even get an error message. Without thinking, he pressed the button again, but he didn't get a response the second time either. He didn't understand what could be wrong with his ship. He had flown it all the way back from Earth only yesterday. It should be ready to fly.

Unless someone had sabotaged him.

He scrambled back down the ramp and underneath the ship. One of the access panels was hanging open, wires dangling from it. A small cylinder lay on the ground below. It must be the starting mechanism.

Troxeo scooped it up and began reattaching it to the wires. In his mind, the disabling of his spacecraft confirmed that Arkhan was the one who had broken Katie out of prison. Something like this was just his style, and he would have known that Troxeo would start pursuit immediately. Anyone else might have damaged all the ships in the yard. When he looked around, he didn't see problems with any of the other vessels. Only his was disabled.

He cursed as he accidentally cut the tip of his finger on an exposed wire. He should be requisitioning another ship, but that would mean informing Commander Reck of his suspicions about Arkhan. He would have to find his superior officer, explain the whole mess, file a report or two, and possibly implicate himself in his unsanctioned interrogation of Katie. By the time he received a new ship through official channels, Arkhan would be long gone.

When he finally had the starting mechanism reattached, Troxeo shoved it back up into the underbelly of the vehicle and slammed the access panel shut. He hoped he hadn't wired it incorrectly in his haste. Back on the bridge, he pressed his left hand on the smooth green panel and punched the red button with his right. The ship whirred to life around him, dash lighting up and the engine roaring. He could finally get out of here.

Troxeo boosted the ship into the air and started tracking nearby signs of life. He scanned the readout screen eagerly, but there was nothing on it. He was too late. Arkhan had already fled out of range.

CHAPTER 19

Katie sat against the back of her seat and breathed a sigh of relief. She hadn't been in her cell for long, but it was enough to make her realize she wasn't interested in staying. The Oretoz had treated her worse than an animal. She didn't even want to imagine what would have happened to her in the future.

Chixo had told her Commander Reck planned to interview her again in the morning. She wondered if he had discovered her absence yet.

Katie pressed her face against the window and watched the land drift further away into the distance underneath her. From this view, she could easily imagine the ship was flying over Earth. The colors were darker here and the buildings were slightly different shapes, but civilization was civilization. There were roads, parks, and clumps of small homes huddled together between them. For everyone else, life was going on as usual despite the fact that their human prisoner had escaped. Katie wondered what was happening back on Earth. Did her parents even know aliens had kidnapped her?

An image of Troxeo flashed across her mind. She tried to stop thinking about him, but he kept looming in front of her eyes. The big man throwing her over his shoulder on the Earth spaceship headed for Bonaan, the curious look on his face when he visited her quarters on his ship, the force with which he ripped off clothing.

What was happening to Troxeo right now? Were they holding him responsible for her escape? Or was he down below her somewhere on a different ship, preparing to follow them and drag her back to the underground prison? She hadn't quite been able to figure out Troxeo and determine whether he was her enemy or something else. There was a spark in his green eyes that she couldn't seem to forget.

"Thank you guys again for getting me out of there," Katie said to Chixo, who sat across from her. Chixo was digging the dirt out from under her nails with a knife. The seats on the small ship ran along the sides instead of facing the front. "I don't know how much longer I could have handled the isolation."

Chixo snorted a little and looked up at the human. "You were hardly in there at all compared to the rest of the prisoners. It's unusual for anyone to return from one of those cells."

"Really? What did the other people do?" Katie had imagined that it would be like the prisons back on Earth, where everyone had a certain amount of time behind bars based on their crimes. But now that she was thinking about it, she had done nothing to merit being placed behind bars.

"All sorts of things. Most of them have spoken out against the Council either in the open or in private." The alien shrugged. "It's just one of those things you're not supposed to do."

Katie leaned forward in her seat. "Really? You're not allowed to say you don't like what your leaders are doing? What if they're wrong about something?"

Chixo looked at her as though she were crazy. "Of course not. It would only breed dissent in our city which would spread to other parts of Oretoz. You're either with the Council or against them. There's no in-between, and they don't tolerate anyone who is against them."

Katie supposed there were regions like that on Earth, but she wasn't from one of them. "That sounds terrible. Well, I can't wait to get back home. I'm ready to curl up in a real bed with a big mug of chamomile tea. Arkhan, how long will it be before we reach Earth?"

Arkhan turned around in his seat next to Enan. "Earth? A long time. Never." He turned back around.

"That's hilarious," Katie retorted. "Really. Do we have to transfer to a different ship somewhere?"

The big man shook his dark head. "Nope. This ship is all we have."

"What are you going on about?" Chixo asked. "We're in a land hopper. You couldn't use it to get outside the atmosphere if you tried. Even if you could, this compartment would depressurize in an instant."

Arkhan turned around again with a strange grin on his face. "We aren't getting a different ship because we don't need one. We aren't going back to Earth."

Katie had thought it would be difficult to get clearance for a flight to Earth. "Are you taking me to Bonaan? It makes sense. I was headed there in the first place. I'm sure I can arrange transportation back to Earth. But it's an entirely different planet. Do you have a way to get there without a ship, like a transporter?"

"We're not going to Bonaan either."

She stared into his dark eyes, and her stomach started to twist. For the first time, she felt like something was wrong. Katie was still wearing the electromagnetic handcuffs Arkhan had slapped on her wrists back in the prison. She wouldn't be able to move her arms unless someone freed her. Chixo had already questioned him about his choice of a ship before they left the Fortress.

"Where are you taking me?" she whispered.

Arkhan stood and came into the back of the hopper. He was too tall to stand up straight in the small ship. He had to bend over when he reached her seat. "You are an intriguing creature and far too interesting to be locked away in a prison cell. But I can't let you go, either, not when I have other plans for you." He ran a thick finger down her cheek. "You are no longer the prisoner of Troxeo or Commander Reck. Now we are free to be with each other."

Katie tried to recoil from his touch, but there wasn't much space to move around. Her head was already against the window behind her. "I don't understand what you mean. Why would you go to all the trouble to help me escape and not take me back home?"

"Because he's an idiot, that's why." Chixo rose from her seat. Unlike Arkhan, she was able to stand up fully. She pointed an angry finger in his face. "I can't believe you. We broke about a dozen military regulations and turned ourselves into outlaws so you could fuck an alien? I would never have helped you if I had known."

"That's being a little harsh, don't you think?" Arkhan put up a weak attempt to feign innocence. "You said yourself that you didn't like her living conditions. I promise you Katie won't be kept in a cell while she is with me. She might end up naked again, though."

Katie launched herself out of her seat. Arkhan had been looking at Chixo, and he didn't have time to react before she slammed the top of her head into his face. She felt his nose crunch against her skull and saw two gushes of blood start to drip down his face.

"You little bitch!" He flung her to the floor of the spaceship.

Stars danced across Katie's vision as she struggled to get to her feet. Arkhan reached for her again, but Chixo distracted him.

"If you lay another hand on her, I'm going to report our location immediately. There'll be a swarm of officers here before you know it." She had her hands on her hips and was doing her best to look threatening despite her small stature. Katie noticed her hand was inching down her side to a blaster.

Arkhan stared down at her with disgust. "You wouldn't do that. You would implicate yourself as well as me. If you call us in, your reward will be a cell right next to mine in the Fortress."

"Let's find out." Chixo's hand rested on her blaster. "Staying in the Fortress would be less of a punishment than working alongside a dishonest soldier."

Arkhan was finished playing around and wanted to get past this obstacle. He pulled a weapon out of his belt and fired it at Chixo, who fell in a crumpled heap on the floor of the ship.

Katie rushed over to the alien woman's side. A tiny needle protruded from her neck, trembling in tune with her pulse. "What did you do?" She could hear the panic in her voice. It was embarrassing, but she had just lost her only ally. Enan was still silently flying the plane. He didn't seem eager to jump to her defense.

"It was only a tranquilizer. I had a feeling she might not see things the same way I do. I'm not going to kill someone I've known and trained with my whole life, but I don't have to let her ruin my plans either."

"What are your plans, exactly?" Katie countered. "What could you possibly want with me?"

Arkhan narrowed his eyes. "Haven't you figured it out yet? You have a certain allure to men from my planet. I guess humans are as stupid as they say. I've seen the way Troxeo looks at you. He might deny it, but I know he sees the same thing I do. It's impossible not to notice the way you hold yourself when you walk and how your curves take over an entire room." He licked his lips as he looked down at her, not meeting her eyes but studying her body. "You seem different from our women. You are soft, and it makes a man hard."

Katie whipped her foot up to kick him in the knee. She would have gone higher if she had been able to reach his balls. "Stay away from me."

The big man didn't seem affected at all by her little attack. He grinned. "That's perfect. I like a challenge. I wouldn't have gone to 'all this trouble' if I didn't. But don't get too feisty, Earthling, or I'll give you a shot just like Chixo. It won't kill you, but it will make you wish you were dead." Katie cringed when he moved toward her, but he walked past to pick up Chixo's limp form. He dragged it toward the back of the ship.

"What are you doing with her?" Katie demanded.

He shot her an irritated look. "Will you stop asking so many irrelevant questions? I'm putting her into an escape pod. She doesn't need to come with us."

He set Chixo down in a particular seat at the back of the ship. It was set apart from the others. There were several buttons on the arm of the chair, and Arkhan pushed a few in a predetermined sequence. When he had pushed the last button, a clear bubble closed over Chixo's body. A flick of a switch opened a hatch in the rear of the plane. The bubble containing Chixo slowly rolled toward the opening, moved down the ramp, and bounced away into the sky.

Katie's face contorted into a silent scream. Arkhan gave her a derisive smile.

"You know she's safe, right? I'm good at protecting people. You'll see. Chixo's in an escape pod. It's on autopilot, and it will take her back to the Fortress. Fortunately for us, they don't move very fast, and she'll probably still be unconscious by the time she arrives. It will take a while for them to wake her up and get the full story out of her. With luck, we will be too far gone for anyone to find us. I'm not sure what she would tell them. She doesn't know where we're going." He flicked the overhead switch and the ramp closed.

Katie's body felt frozen, but her mind whirred. If Arkhan just sent Chixo back to the capital while she was comatose, they might not blame her for what happened. She hoped she would look more like a victim than a conspirator.

Arkhan stepped around her and took his seat at the front of the ship once again. "I suggest you make yourself comfortable. It's going to be a while before we arrive."

CHAPTER 20

Troxeo slammed his fists onto his ship's console. Katie wasn't any better off in Arkhan's hands than she would have been in the prison. Knowing him, she might be in a worse position. What would he do to her? He already knew the answer to his hypothetical question. Troxeo remembered all too vividly the way his cousin had eyed the Earthling, and the conversation they held afterward. He knew what Arkhan would do to Katie.

Arkhan wanted the Earth girl as badly as Troxeo did, but they had different motivations. Arkhan merely wanted to take his pleasure from her soft, rounded flesh and use her like he used everyone else in life. Troxeo swore Arkhan wouldn't get the opportunity to have his way with Katie if he ever got to see her again. He wanted her flesh as well, but he wanted even more than that. He ran his hands through his hair. He should never have let Arkhan help with his mission to Earth, no matter what their blood ties were.

The problem now was figuring out their destination. His spaceship was headed east because he had seen the hopper go in that direction. But Troxeo knew the initial heading of a ship wasn't an accurate indicator of its final destination. Where could Arkhan possibly take her that would be safe from the prying eyes of a pursuing military force? The city stretched for miles around the Fortress. There were a few small towns to the east of Capital City, but after that, there was nothing but woods.

Then it hit him. Arkhan had taken a hopper because he didn't plan on leaving the planet. He broke Katie out of prison, but he wasn't going to return her to Earth. He was going to keep her for himself. There was only one place Troxeo imagined he could go. He changed the course of his ship and turned the engines up to full speed.

Several generations ago, before the Oretoz had united under the Council, Troxeo's family had been farmers. They had lived their lives peacefully in the country, but they were always willing to stand up for what they thought was right. His family had been ideal candidates to become soldiers once the alliance had formed. The Council heavily recruited for its new army and promised excellent pay.

The Trepniss men and women signed up without hesitation, and their children and their children's children continued to serve the Council as they came of age. Eventually, the agrarian home in the country was forgotten. There was no need for it when soldiers began staying close to their commanders in case duty called. They lived in the Capital City now, bunking with their brothers and sisters in arms.

Troxeo remembered the old homestead and knew Arkhan did, as well. As children, they had convinced one of their relatives to take them there in a beat-up land ship. Over time, trees had begun to creep closer to the old building and it had been vacant for many years. Undeterred, they broke in through the back door and explored the old house.

Dry Oretoz air had preserved the building and its contents. They shared a laugh at the simple tools of their ancestors and their clothing. Troxeo was old enough to remember there was a lack of communication devices built into the house, unlike modern homes. There wasn't even the luxury of elevator pods. Instead, there was a dangerous-looking tall and complicated structure built of wood that required a man to use his feet to reach the next level of the house. Wood had fallen out of favor as a building material. His grandfather had told him about an incredible boom in technology after the Council took over. Many of the old homes were never upgraded.

Troxeo knew the old homestead would have a magnetic appeal for Arkhan. There were no communicators, no surveillance systems, and nobody else around for miles. Or at least there wouldn't be until Troxeo found them. He hoped his childhood memories would be a good enough guide to find the old place. It wasn't on any of the maps.

He put his hand on his ship's built-in communicator, then slowly lifted it off again. He knew what he was supposed to do. He should call it into the Fortress. A dutiful soldier would let Commander Reck know the situation right away, either directly or through his subordinates.

Troxeo's responsibility was informing Reck that he suspected Arkhan was the one who had stolen the prisoner. He needed to request backup ships. Any prison escapee was a big deal, especially one from another planet. If he were able to recapture Katie successfully, Reck might even be in a good enough mood to give Troxeo a promotion. That was all he had hoped for by bringing the Earthling to Reck in the first place.

It was his duty, but Troxeo couldn't perform it. He stared at the communicator for a few moments, unsure of what to do. If he captured Katie and brought her back, she would be put into cell 406 again, if she were lucky. It was likely Commander Reck would order him to kill her on sight. He imagined the beautiful woman's face contorted in fear and confusion as he shot her. He wouldn't do it.

He reached for the communicator again, but he turned it off instead of activating it. There no question in his mind as to why he was doing this. His purpose was clear. He was going to rescue Katie. He had to know if she was his eleste.

CHAPTER 21

Katie slumped in her seat. The cityscape below had vanished long ago, giving way to a thick forest of trees. At another time, they might have been beautiful, with shimmering emerald leaves that blended into a strip of green across the countryside. Today she didn't have enough energy to enjoy it. She was running out of hope.

If Katie had the reach she would have kicked herself for sending her application to TerraMates. Would being a mail-order bride on an alien planet have fixed any of her problems? She thought Ben had ruined her life by cheating on her, but it turned out she had ruined it herself by getting onto a spaceship headed for Bonaan. If she had spent some time at her parents' place to get herself together, she might never have been in this situation.

She wondered if her family would ever find out what happened to her.

"Is this the place?" Enan murmured from the front. Arkhan nodded, and the ship began a quick descent.

Katie watched as they rushed toward the treetops. Her stomach lurched in time to the movements of the hopper as they approached a small clearing. She had never been afraid of flying before, but she didn't enjoy landing. It didn't matter if she was on an airplane or a spaceship. It always seemed to Katie like they were on the verge of crashing into the ground. Enan and Arkhan had experience as pilots, but that fact didn't make her feel any better. She didn't have a reason to trust either one of them.

Anger bubbled inside of her as she thought about Arkhan again. The bloody nose she gave him had been the least of what he deserved. He had told her he would help her, but abducting her was about as far from providing assistance as possible. It turned out that men from any planet could be deceptive.

The hopper landed with a thump and the exotic foliage rushed past her window. The hopper steadily slowed before coming to a jolting halt just before the forest walled off a clearing in front of them.

Arkhan rose from his seat and entered the back of the ship. He grabbed Katie by the elbow and hauled her upright. "Are you ready for a little hike?"

They marched down the ramp of the hopper, and it closed behind them. Katie heard the spaceship start. She tried to turn back and look at the ship. Arkhan, however, continued to drag her toward the woods. The shadow of the land hopper spread over the clearing as the vehicle flew back up into the sky.

"Where's Enan going?" she asked. "Isn't he coming with us?"

Arkhan laughed darkly. It was an ominous sound that was absorbed quickly by the vegetation around them. "Do you have any idea how long it takes that man to dislodge himself from the cockpit of a small ship? He had to get up before dawn just to make sure he was ready on time. I don't need him anymore."

"All right, then where are we going?" They had stepped into the tree line. The tall, straight trunks of the trees surrounded them like a pack of guardians, and their leafy tops nearly blocked out the sunlight. The undergrowth wasn't dense. It consisted of vines with arrow-shaped leaves.

Arkhan pulled on her arm, interrupting her survey of the scene. "Let's just say we're going to an old family home. It's the perfect spot for a secluded romantic retreat."

"I think you read my mind. Nothing says 'romance' like electromagnetic handcuffs and dragging me through the woods." Katie stumbled as a vine caught her toe. Chixo had given her a slim pair of boots to wear with her bodysuit. They seemed to be made of the same slick material but had slightly hardened soles. The shoes fit well and were comfortable, but weren't suited for a nature trek. "Can you slow down a little?"

The muscled alien soldier pulled a large knife out of a sheath on his belt and slashed through a web of vines growing between the trees. "No."

"Then can you at least take off these handcuffs? It's hard to keep my balance when I'm running through a forest without being able to use my hands." She tripped again, running to keep up with him on the uneven floor.

"I don't think so."

"It's not like you'd have to worry about me running off, you know. Where will I go on an alien planet? Do you think I'm fast enough to outrun you and smart enough to survive in these woods without you? I appreciate your confidence, but the simple truth is I'm not."

Katie did have some survival experience. Her father used to drag her out on camping trips long past the age at which it was still cool to hang out with your parents. She had secretly enjoyed the vacations, but she had always told her friends how boring they were. The truth was that she liked cooking hot dogs over the campfire and sleeping under the stars. He had also managed to teach her some excellent survival skills along the way. Of course, whether or not she would be able to apply them to a different world was an unanswered question.

"Stop trying to talk your way out of this, Katie. I made up my mind to free you from that cell and keep you for myself. I know what my future holds if I go back there. By now, I've lost my position in the military and have become an outlaw." He plowed through the forest with ease as though he had done this many times before.

"It doesn't have to be that way. Surely you haven't gone so far that you can't redeem yourself." Katie wasn't sure how it would help her if Arkhan decided to take her back to the Fortress. She knew she would be under such heavy security that she would have no chance of getting out a second time. Katie would be lucky if they didn't kill her on sight. She couldn't help talking to Arkhan. It brought a sense of reality to the dreamlike experience.

Arkhan halted and turned to face her. He squeezed her elbow tightly as he spoke. "Don't even think you can make me change my mind. What's done is done." He faced forward again and continued marching.

After a while, Katie began to wonder how long the hike was going to last. Her feet were sore, and her stomach growled like a bear. Arkhan, however, didn't seem affected by the journey. Eventually, the trees started to thin out, and she could see bits and pieces of a structure. It was hard to tell with the trees obscuring it, but it seemed like a large home.

Wide windows in the walls reflected the forest. Wood paneling that had lost its paint long ago surrounded the glass. The boards sagged, and several of them were barely hanging on to the structure. In all, the place was still standing but extremely dilapidated. It was the kind of place Katie imagined seeing in a documentary about serial killers. The house once had a large yard around it. The tree trunks here weren't as large, but the branches had done their best to encroach on the old building. Ropes of vines crawled up the sides of the building and pried their way between wooden boards.

"What is this place?" She knew her face was curled up in a look of disgust, but she didn't care. Arkhan could kiss her ass at this point.

"This was the old family homestead. My grandparents were the last ones in my family to live here before everyone moved to the Capital City. Nobody has thought about it much since then, which is why it's perfect."

Katie's stomach churned. "Perfect for what?"

"For us to live. It looks bad on the outside, but you'd be surprised how well Oretoz construction stands up over time. Besides, it's old-fashioned. I understand humans like that." Arkhan tipped his head back to look up at the place with reverence.

Katie would have argued with him, but she was too busy looking behind her. The leaf litter on the forest floor was thick, and she and Arkhan had made loud crunching noises in it on their way here. The woods were silent now, but Katie thought there were sounds of another set of steps in the detritus. Arkhan tugged at her arm, but she resisted. "Did you hear that?" she whispered.

Arkhan looked as though he wanted to argue with her and tell her to stop changing the subject. Surprisingly, he restrained himself and listened for a moment. Silence met their ears.

"Nice try."

"No, really." Her whisper had become a regular speaking voice and sounded urgent now. "I heard something." As she listened again, she realized what a fool she had been. If someone was out there with them, there was a chance they were here to rescue her.

"Nobody has been here for years. Everyone lives in towns now, not in the countryside." He tugged on her arm again, harder this time.

Katie pitched forward as she stumbled after him, regaining her footing before she collapsed. They approached the house and eased their way up the front steps. Several of them had rotted away in various places, with holes showing the darkness below. The deck on the covered porch was in slightly better condition, having more protection from the elements. "Looks like it needs more than a coat of paint," she muttered.

"Shut up." Arkhan crossed the porch carefully and tried the front door. The knob turned smoothly, and the door swung open with ease. He raised an eyebrow and lowered his voice to a whisper. "Someone has been here recently." He looked behind them, scrutinizing the copse of trees they had passed to reach the house.

Katie felt a pulse of fear race up her spine. Faced with a danger she knew and danger she didn't know, it was hard to tell which one gave better odds for survival. It didn't help that she had the distinct feeling someone was watching her.

Finding nothing in the yard, Arkhan stepped through the doorway, pulling Katie behind him. He moved silently despite the heavy boots on his feet, looking in every direction before advancing.

The house was dark on the inside because the tree leaves blocked the sunlight. Despite the darkness, Katie could tell they stood in a wide foyer. The remnants of a rug which had deteriorated into a web of threads stretched underneath their feet. A light fixture dangled from a wire overhead. It was a tangled mass of metal which threatened to come crashing down on them at any moment. Hulking shadows in the corners indicated the shells of furniture. Leaves had drifted in from an open window somewhere. The breeze from the door made the leaves move around the floor like small, terrified animals.

A creaking noise sounded above them, and Arkhan pushed her back into the shadow of the door. He pulled a blaster from his belt and held it at shoulder height. The creaking paused, then resumed with determination, turning into the sound of footsteps. A figure appeared at the top of the stairs. Its features were indistinguishable in the dim light.

"Bayo, are you here?" the unknown person said before descending the stairs at a rapid pace. "I didn't expect you back for days. I didn't think you would find it so…"

His words were cut off in midsentence when Arkhan fired a shot into his chest. His weapon barely made a noise as he pulled the trigger. A burning blue light illuminated the entrance wound. The figure fell, sliding down the remaining stairs on his back. Arkhan trotted up to it, but Katie stayed where she was in the corner.

"A squatter," Arkhan said as he looked over the body. "I should have known."

"I thought you said nobody lived out here." She didn't want to look at the pale face in the dim light, but it was hard not to. He had the same broad build as all the other males on this planet, but he lacked a robust set of muscles to fill it out. A square jaw and prominent cheekbones accentuated the hollow face. His clothing hung on him, looking ragged from being torn and patched repeatedly.

The soldier shrugged. "I'd heard rumors, but I didn't believe them. I'll have to be on the lookout for his partner."

"I'm guessing that wasn't a tranquilizer dart." A pool of blood had started forming around the man, dripping slowly down the stairs. She wondered who he was and what he had been doing here.

"No, it wasn't." Arkhan left the body for a moment and came back to her. He grabbed her arms and pulled her to the banister of the stairs, too close to the body of the stranger for her comfort. He manipulated the handcuffs in ways she couldn't see in the darkness, and quickly she found herself attached to the stair rail by the restraints. "You're going to stay here while I take care of this body."

Katie nodded, having no choice. Her scalp crawled at the idea that the other squatter might show up. She could only hope that he or she was a friendly person, and knew how to get her out of these damn handcuffs. Then again, the stranger could be worse than Arkhan. At least he seemed to want to keep her alive.

Arkhan picked up the body by the ankles and dragged it out the front door, leaving a dark trail of blood in his wake.

CHAPTER 22

Troxeo had pushed his ship to the limit. He had to get to the homestead before anything happened to Katie. In the dark depths of his brain, he was worried Arkhan hadn't waited to reach his destination before carrying out his disgusting plan. He could see Katie on the floor of the land hopper, pinned down under the bulk of his cousin. She was screaming and struggling against him, but she was no match for Arkhan. That left Chixo piloting the ship, and Troxeo wondered what Arkhan had promised her.

He tried to move the whole scenario out of his mind.

For now, his primary focus had to be on rescuing Katie. He was certain Arkhan was headed for the country, even though there wasn't a trace of the land hopper on any of his screens. He still remembered the layout of the land and the arrangement of the house. Arkhan's only advantage was time. Troxeo was determined to find the human and get her away from Arkhan. He was willing to do whatever was required.

But if he found her, what was the next step? He couldn't take her back to the Fortress in Capital City. If he returned her to Earth, he ran the risk of having her leap off his ship and never interacting with him again. It would also expose the existence of Oretoz to Earth, ruining any chance of a surprise attack. He would have to find another option, and he would have to convince her he wasn't her enemy. Troxeo had acted in ways Katie could misinterpret, so he had quite a challenge in front of him.

Looking down, Troxeo recognized the river that zigzagged through the trees, splitting them like a crack in a green gemstone. It wasn't far now. He lowered the ship slightly, searching for a clearing in which to land. One appeared in the trees ahead of his position. Scorch marks on the grass told him another spacecraft had recently landed here.

Troxeo brought his ship to a gentle landing in the little meadow, stopping well before the burnt tracks of the land hopper. He wondered where it went and who was flying it. Had Chixo taken the spacecraft in another direction to throw him off the scent?

He disembarked and headed into the woods. It had been a long time since he felt the grass under his feet or breathed in the fresh air of the country. The Capital City had numerous air recycling plants, but the air out here tasted different. Unfortunately, Troxeo didn't have enough time to enjoy the experience. He pressed onward, determined to get to Katie as quickly as possible. His hands touched his blaster and the handles of his knives every few minutes, reassuring him that they were still there.

After several minutes of walking, Troxeo stopped. He heard something rustling in the leaf litter, but the noise stopped as soon as he started listening to it. Whenever he advanced, the noise stopped. Whoever was out here didn't want anyone tracking them. It was impossible to walk silently on the thick carpet of dried leaves.

He walked on, watching the trees around him for any sign of an ambush. It would be smart of Arkhan to wait for him somewhere in the woods and attack before he reached the house. But everything seemed clear ahead of him. The noise sounded like it was coming from the rear.

He stopped and whirled around, but whatever made the noise was too fast for him. It must have hidden somewhere, camouflaged by the trees. He moved on, eager to either find Arkhan or finish his encounter in the woods.

A battle cry sounded behind him. Troxeo whipped his knife out of its sheath as he spun around, only to slash at thin air when he wildly swung his weapon at chest height. The attacker was too low for the strike he planned to sink in the heart of a man. Instead, the form barreled into his knees, knocking him into the leaf litter.

Troxeo couldn't see his enemy at first. It moved quickly, plowing into him repeatedly as he tried to get up. He struck out blindly with his knife, burying it into the body of his foe. His hand ran through thick, matted hair.

Something sharp slashed into Troxeo's calf. He felt burning as his blood spilled onto the detritus of the forest, but he had to keep fighting. The assailant didn't give him time to grab his other weapons. He was too close to use his blaster even if he had been able to pull it out of its holster.

His new enemy was relentless and seemed to target every part of his body simultaneously. Stabs of pain rang out from his legs and torso as he struggled to push the heavy body away. He yanked his knife out of his opponent's flesh and stabbed upward once again. This time, he was rewarded with a rush of warm blood over his arm. The weight of his antagonist sagged against him, and Troxeo pushed violently against the mass.

It didn't rise again.

Troxeo turned his head and found himself face-to-face with a long, slimy snout. It had a large white tusk on either side, blood dripping from one of them. Troxeo pulled himself to a sitting position so he could better see the dead beast. It had a skinny, hairy body with four legs ending in pointed hooves. The weapons on the animal's feet explained how it was able to attack its prey thoroughly. It must have been stomping on Troxeo while also trying to gore him. The creature had dark, beady eyes that were now staring blankly at the forest floor. A knife protruded out of its neck.

He had heard of the wild creatures in the forest before but had never seen one himself. The beast had been harder to fight off than a sentient being, whose moves he could anticipate and counter. Fighting a man was nothing like fighting a wild animal. He couldn't attack it at its center of gravity or intimidate it with words.

Troxeo stood and looked down at the creature. In any other circumstance, he would have taken its tusks as a trophy. Today, however, he had two other concerns that took precedence. One was getting to Katie on time. The other was a large gash in his leg leaving a bright crimson stain on the dead leaves behind him.

He reached into the pocket of his pants and pulled out a small case. Troxeo had only used this kit once before, and that had been a long time ago. Typically Troxeo received treatment from a medic, not a primitive field kit. He pulled the needle and a length of thread from the case, but his hands were shaking too much from adrenaline for him to insert the end of the thread through the needle. The injury was too significant to glue shut. He took deep breaths to calm down before he was able to use the needle.

It was hard to sew his cut closed due to the oozing blood, but he had no choice. Troxeo maneuvered into an awkward position to get at the right angle. He held his skin together with his left hand while wielding the needle with his right. He imagined he presented an awkward picture to any observers. He was a trained soldier in the middle of the woods, tending to a wound from a wild creature. It felt like he was living in a history book.

Knotting the thread and returning the needle to its case, Troxeo slowly rose to his feet. The stitching made his leg tight, and it was hard to walk. He couldn't let mere physical discomfort or his blood loss stop him now. He bent to retrieve his knife from the animal's throat before continuing into the woods.

When he came to the house, he paused. He watched it from a distance for a minute, hoping to see if there was any movement from Arkhan. The place seemed quiet and empty, just as he imagined it would be after years of abandonment. The forest had overtaken more of it than when Troxeo had been here as a child. Other than that, it was exactly as haunting and decrepit as he remembered.

Between the vines and tree branches, Troxeo could see the front door was standing open.

CHAPTER 23

Katie tugged at the handcuffs over her head that kept her fastened to the banister. Her arms were beginning to tingle as the blood drained out of them. She looked around at the house, searching for anything that might help her. There wasn't much to see in the dim light, and there certainly weren't any weapons within reach.

Arkhan came back through the front door a few minutes later, wiping his hands on the sides of his pants. "What did you do with him?" she asked.

"You are far too curious for your own good, Earthling. But if you must know, I dragged the body out where the animals would get rid of it for me. I don't want it stinking up our love nest, after all."

"Don't call it that. I'll never love you," she spat.

"No? But you wanted to be a mail-order bride, didn't you?" He was standing in front of her now, looking down into her face with piercing eyes. "I pulled you out of prison, and now I'm helping make your wish come true. Does it matter if you belong to me instead of a Bonaan that doesn't know what to do with a woman?" He touched her cheek, but she turned away from him. "None of this has to be difficult."

"If it doesn't, then why am I still in these handcuffs? Are you not talented enough to keep hold of me without them?"

Katie should have held her tongue. It was the wrong thing to say. Arkhan's hand smacked into the side of her face with a loud pop. He wrapped his fingers around her throat and forced her to look up at him. "Do you want to challenge me? I can show you how strong I am right now, if you'd like." Arkhan stepped back and began pacing in front of her. "Tell me something, human. What do you call two people that mate for life on your planet?"

"We get married. We become husband and wife." The words nearly caught in her throat as she became choked up. At one point, she thought she would be getting married to Ben. As rotten as he turned out to be, at least he had never chained her to the stairs.

"That's right! I remember reading about that. Troxeo didn't do any extra work, but I researched your planet a little myself before we set out to capture you. As I recall, you spend a lot of time filling out paperwork and planning ceremonies." His smile went cold as he paused to look at her. "You don't have to worry about any of that here. We like to get down to business."

"You forget a crucial element," Katie retorted.

"Really? Please, enlighten me."

"The two people have to want to be together. The only thing I want right now is for you to go away." Katie was lying. She also wanted to get out of the handcuffs. They were beginning to dig into her wrists.

Arkhan shook his head and gave a deep laugh. "That's where you're wrong, human. I have a big empty house. There are no witnesses around us. I have a sexy Earth creature at my disposal, and I have a desire for her. As for the other thing you mentioned? I'm sure I can make you change your mind."

"You've done a piss-poor job of convincing me so far." She tried to wiggle her fingers, but her hands had gone numb. She couldn't tell if she was moving anything. Arkhan was close to her now. She could feel the heat of his body against her and his foul breath on her face.

Without warning, Arkhan pressed his lips over her mouth. She tried to move away but couldn't pull her head back any further because of the stairs. When she tried to shift her head, he forced his hands on either side of her face, holding it still. Eventually, he pulled away, licking his lips. "That was a shame. It could have been more pleasant for you if you had only cooperated a little. Do you know anything about our ways and customs here, Earthling?"

"Why would I give a shit?"

He gave her a wicked grin again. "It looks like you have some time on your hands, so I'll be merciful and educate you. On my planet, where you are right now, the males can mate with any woman that wishes to, whenever we want and without any of your silly documentation and vows. We meet, we fuck, and we go on about our lives."

Katie wanted to challenge him, but she was getting too tired to bother. The energy pill Chixo had given her back at the prison had worn off while they were still on the land hopper. She could feel exhaustion starting to take over her body.

"Sometimes, though, we find a woman who is too good to share with others. I haven't found one for myself yet. There can be a special bond between two people. It's something that possesses you and makes you ignore everything else in your life for the favor of a single woman. I've certainly done that for you, haven't I? I want you so badly that I've changed my entire life. Surely it must mean something?"

"Yep. It means you're crazy."

Arkhan slapped her again, and she sagged against the banister. He grabbed her by the hips and hoisted her back up, pressing himself against her. She could feel the hard bulge of his cock between his thighs, but she didn't have the strength to break his tight grip. He pressed his mouth down on her again. This time, she clamped her lips together to avoid his prying tongue.

"I want you, and I mean to have you. I'm not wasting any more time." He removed the handcuffs from the rail but left them attached to her body. The big man pulled her around to the front of the stairs and walked up, yanking her along behind him.

Katie's mind was beginning to fog over. She felt like things were moving in slow motion as she watched Arkhan's boot press down into the trail of blood left by the squatter. When his foot reached the next stair and lifted up again, it left a faint trace of red. It looked like a giant rubber stamp, marking the path to her doom.

She didn't have the strength to lift her foot to follow him. Arkhan gave a quick tug to her arm that sent her sprawling on the sharp edges of the stairs. The pain jolted life back into her body. Determined to fight back, she wrapped her ankles around one of the spindles holding up the railing.

Arkhan turned, bemused to see her latest attempt to delay the inevitable. "Unless you want to break your delicate ankles, I suggest you let go." He wrenched her arm to prove his point. Katie's heels fell to the ground with twin thuds.

He dragged her up the stairs on her ass. From her position, Katie could see the fading light of the front door. She stared numbly at the door as it receded from her gaze.

CHAPTER 24

The big house was eerily quiet. The thumps of Katie's heels echoed through the halls as Arkhan dragged her up the last few steps. If her life were a movie, she imagined this would be the scary part with dramatic music playing. She would have appreciated a background soundtrack. As it turned out, the oppressive silence was more terrifying than she had ever imagined.

What would happen to her in Arkhan's hands? She knew he wanted to fuck her, of course, but what did that mean with someone from Oretoz? And what would happen to her? He made things sound like their arrangement would be a long-term situation, but would he let her live? Would she want to?

She had the opportunity to throw herself down the steps, but something prevented her. She still had a faint hope that she would survive.

When they reached the top of the stairs, Arkhan's steps slowed. Katie was in the middle of a long hallway with multiple doorways on either side. Some of the doors stood open, allowing in the faint light which could penetrate through the heavy forest outside. Others were about to fall off their hinges, creating jagged shadows on the wall. There seemed to be no color in the building. Katie wondered if Oretoz preferred to decorate minimally or if the house had once been colorful and had faded over time.

Heading to the left, Arkhan looked into several rooms, deciding which one would be the best for a romantic afternoon fuck. Katie could have gotten her feet back underneath her, but she consented to being dragged. There was no point in fighting Arkhan or cooperating with him. Either way, her fate would be the same.

"Here we are," he said. Arkhan had finally decided on a room, pulling Katie through a doorway. "The master suite. It's the perfect place for a new couple. I suggest you familiarize yourself with the ceiling in this room, Earthling, because you'll see it a lot." He closed the door behind them with a thud of finality.

Katie looked over her shoulder to take in her surroundings. A huge bed occupied most of the floor space. The original blankets still lay on it, looking dusty and ragged. Several pieces of furniture stood in the corners. They were enormous hulks of wood covered with elaborate carvings. Either the heat or the humidity had gotten to them long ago, making drawers and doors hang at odd angles, appearing to be evil eyes and crooked grins. The remains of a rug dotted the wooden floor underneath her. Though it might once have been grand, the suite was now the exact opposite of a romantic room.

She scoffed. "What a beautiful place to get away and relax. Is anyone in charge of condemning disgusting places like this?"

Arkhan yanked on the handcuffs, pulling Katie to her feet and making the metal dig further into her wrists. "I don't want to hear any more of your lip, human. From now on, your job is to stay silent unless I ask something of you." He stood over her, face inches away from her mouth, showing a horrifying mix of anger and passion.

She glared back at him angrily, rising to his challenge. "Make me."

The big man pulled out a small cylinder from a belt pouch and pressed it against her ribs. A shock rippled through her body, making her feel like something was punching her from the inside. The sensation only lasted for a moment, but the feeling didn't leave her body even after he removed the device from her skin.

"That's the lowest setting, and it was working through your clothing. I have no problem using it to keep you in line. I can turn it all the way from mildly painful to extremely painful. I've warned you over and over to do as I say. I suppose I've been too kind to you. It might take you longer to realize your desire for me this way, but you'll get there."

Katie didn't agree with anything he said. Nobody cound be considered kind who helped capture a woman, then broke her out of prison to turn her into his personal sex slave. She bit her lip to keep from arguing. She didn't want to be shocked again.

Arkhan studied her lips. "I know you wanted to say something, but you didn't. That's sexy. You're starting to get the hang of things already." He reached down and yanked off the covers on the bed, sending swirls of dust into the air. The sheets underneath looked as clean as they could be after years of neglect. "Get in. It's like we're newlyweds."

Katie slowly lowered herself onto the edge of the mattress. It creaked heavily under her weight, and she wondered if it would even hold her alone, much less both of them.

"Don't be shy. Move all the way in," Arkhan urged. He watched her eagerly, licking his lips. "I guess it's all right if you go slowly like that. We can make it last as long as you would like. We have a lifetime together."

She gingerly lay back against the flat pillow, hands pinned in front of her by the restraints. Looking up at him, Arkhan seemed even taller than he had before. She could see the outline of his erection in the front of his pants, a telltale sign of what was to come.

Arkhan's voice sounded husky. "Now I'm finally going to take off your handcuffs. Don't make the mistake of thinking you can escape. I'm stronger and faster than you are. But I don't want those damn things to get between us." He touched the restraints, and they instantly stopped holding together. At another touch, they fell away from her wrists. He picked them up and replaced them on his belt.

"Please." Katie knew she was pleading shamelessly, but she didn't care. Her wrists were sore. Although her hands were free and she could theoretically try to run away, she knew his words were true. He could overpower her in an instant. There would be no escape for her now.

"You're already begging for it, I see. I knew you would change your mind."

Katie hastily amended her words. "Please *don't*. Please don't do this." Katie felt too weak to fight him off physically. He had already proved impossible to sway with words alone, but she couldn't help resisting.

Arkhan wagged the small cylinder in front of her face. "Nope. I said you shouldn't speak. Begging me to make love to you is permissible, but no more talk about putting off the inevitable. It won't work, and it's only going to kill the mood." He climbed onto the bed, hovering above her on his hands and knees. "Right now you want to leave. Before you know it, you'll be begging to make sweet love to me. We'll stay here together, just the two of us. Your pleasure will be so intense that you'll do anything to return the favor to me."

Tears poured out of the corners of Katie's eyes and trickled onto the sheets.

Arkhan nodded. "I can even make you come so hard that you'll cry. It's time to get started." He sat back on his heels, using his weight to pin her legs against the bed. "This bodysuit looks gorgeous on you, but I happen to know there's something more beautiful underneath. You really shouldn't hide yourself."

Katie cringed, expecting him to rip the thin fabric from her body like Troxeo had back at the Fortress. Instead, he leaned down and gripped the collar of the bodysuit in his teeth. His breath felt hot on her neck. She pressed her head into the pillow in revulsion, trying to find a way not to inhale the aroma. His cock pushed against her, but there was nothing she could do to get away from it.

He leisurely pulled the material down Katie's body. It ripped slowly, agonizingly revealing her skin inch by inch. He groaned as he pulled it down past her chest, exposing one creamy breast. Against her will, her nipple hardened in the cold air, standing firm despite her horror. When Arkhan had pulled the bodysuit down to her waist, he spat out the piece he had been holding in his teeth and grinned down at her.

"I see you're ready. Be patient, my little human. I have more work to do." Reaching up to her neckline with his mouth once again, he pulled down the other side of the bodysuit top.

Katie gulped as she lay half-naked on the bed, most of her assets exposed to the prying gaze of the alien man. Ripping clothes off with one's teeth was exactly the kind of thing Ben used to do, that lying, cheating scumbag. He loved doing things the dirty way. Ben had ripped the buttons off her favorite blouses as soon as she came in the door after work. Once, he pulled down her yoga pants and fucked her from behind while she was talking on the phone.

It had been nothing but sex with Ben. She had done whatever he asked: fucked in their friend's guest room at a Super Bowl party, touched herself while he watched, let him come on her face, bend over and take it in the ass. She never told him no, no matter how she felt about it or how tired she was. She had been his sex slave and not even realized it. He had even convinced her that she did those things for him because she loved him. She had been so upset to find that he had cheated on her that she was ready to break up with him immediately. As it turned out, he was no better than the aliens. She just hadn't been smart enough to realize it.

"Your breasts are amazing. Once I'm done removing your outfit, I'm going to suck on them until I'm blue in the face. Then it will be your turn to suck on me." He grabbed the remains of her ensemble and slowly pulled them away from her waist.

CHAPTER 25

Troxeo stood in front of the house, watching and hoping he was wrong about Arkhan. There was no evidence he had come here other than the scorch marks in the clearing. For all Troxeo knew, Arkan had created a clever diversion to get his pursuers lost in the woods while he whisked Katie off to a different place.

He frowned. The beast Troxeo encountered in the woods had taken its toll on him. The gash the creature tore into Troxeo's leg had also managed to nick a blood vessel. He thought he would live, but there was darkness on the edge of his vision. He fought through the pain, determined that nothing would stop him from finding Katie.

The forest seemed to speak to him as he watched the building. Birds sang in the canopy, playing chipper tunes that didn't match his mood. Insects buzzed around him, curious about the newcomer.

The natural sounds would have been interesting if he was on a vacation, but what Troxeo was truly listening for was a sound that would tell him where Arkhan and Katie were. It might be a rustling in the brush or a scream. Anything might indicate he was on the right track. The front door of the house stood ajar, its dark rectangle silently mocking him.

Troxeo double-checked his blaster to make sure he had fully charged it and the safety was disengaged. If Arkhan were really in the house, any situation where he needed to draw his weapon would probably be too close to use it safely. Still, he wanted to be prepared for any situation. With a sigh, Troxeo headed toward the house. He would never know for sure until he went inside.

He slipped through the brush as quietly as possible, stepping down on his toes first and avoiding any fallen branches that might snap underneath him. He kept behind the trees in case Arkhan was watching through one of the many windows. Despite Troxeo's precautions, he knew Arkhan was a trained soldier too. Avoiding detection would be difficult.

As he approached, there was no indication that anyone inside had spotted him. Arkhan didn't come charging out the door or start shooting from an upper window. Was Arkhan hiding in the forest behind him? The idea didn't seem bold enough.

Sometimes Troxeo was disgusted they were from the same family, and yet that was the one thing that had helped him in his search for Katie. Nobody else would have known about this old family home or guess Arkhan fled here.

Troxeo's heart pounded in his chest when he noticed the leaves on the path leading up to the house had been disturbed. He wasn't an expert on the wilderness, but he knew enough to tell the difference between leaves that had been walked on and those that had been blown about by the wind.

His stomach twisted at the thought of seeing Katie again. He had to fight down his rage at knowing that Arkhan kidnaped her. There was no telling what Arkhan was about to do to Katie or had done already. In Troxeo's mind, she looked soft and vulnerable.

Would Arkhan have already had his way with her on the hopper, or would he have waited until he arrived at the house? Would Katie ever be able to accept Troxeo after what Arkhan had done to her? Was the human capable of distinguishing the two men?

Killing Arkhan wasn't out of the question if his cousin had ruined Katie for Troxeo.

Scenarios flashed through his mind, a nightmare developing faster than he could control it. He imagined walking into the house and finding his cousin on top of the human, pumping away at her while she smiled up at him blissfully. She would look at Troxeo, point her finger at him, and tell him to get out. Arkhan would have already convinced Katie that he was the one she wanted, in the charming way he always seemed to have with women. Katie would be Arkhan's forever, and there wouldn't be anything Troxeo could do.

He wondered if the situation was that bad. He tried to swallow the idea, but his mind wouldn't stop working. This time, he saw himself finding Katie held captive but alive. Troxeo would dispose of his cousin with no regrets. The human would be grateful, pressing her curvy body against his as she turned up her velvety lips for a kiss. She would let him or even ask him to take her away from here.

Troxeo crept up the porch stairs, avoiding holes that were big enough to swallow one of his boots easily. The boards creaked as he walked on them. He hoped the breeze was enough to cover the sound. Troxeo felt his blood thrumming in his veins as he approached the front door, prepared for an attack at any moment.

Stepping inside, Troxeo quickly pressed himself against a wall. His heart beat so loudly that it thundered in his ears and seemed as though it would echo through the house. At first, he heard nothing but the rustle of dry leaves as they blew across the porch behind him. The house both sounded and looked empty. He couldn't explain why but he thought someone was there.

Finally, up the stairs and off to his left, Troxeo thought he heard something. It wasn't a sound he could ultimately define or describe. It was more of a muffled ripple of noise that indicated life. It could have been an animal that climbed through a hole in the wall, or a piece of flimsy furniture which fell over in the breeze from a broken window. A fire in his heart told him neither one of the possible explanations was the right one. His eleste was up there waiting for him.

He looked with disgust at the long staircase separating him from the second floor of the house. Troxeo couldn't remember the last time he had to use such an archaic invention. His freshly stitched calf would have preferred using an elevation pod.

Troxeo hoisted himself onto the first step, wincing when a stab of pain ripped through his leg. Gritting his teeth, Troxeo continued, pushing through the pain and letting it fuel his rage. The thing he wanted more than anything was close but beyond his grasp. He was willing to do much more for Katie than climb stairs on a wounded leg.

He dared not lean on the banister for support; several of the balusters were missing or broken. It wouldn't help either of them if he tumbled back down to the ground floor, injuring himself further and calling attention to his presence. Instead, he carefully inched forward as quickly as he dared, shifting his weight off his wounded leg when possible.

When he reached the top, he took a moment to breathe. He braved looked down at his pants leg. A dark stain marred the drab material. He would need a coagulant eventually. Proper treatment would have to wait until he returned to his ship with Katie in his arms.

Troxeo looked down both sides of the long hallway. When he was a child and his grandparents hosted large dinner parties, his parents had told him there were enough bedrooms to house everyone in the family. He had never quite grasped the purpose of a dinner party, but as he looked he realized there were too many rooms to count.

More rooms were around the corner where the hallway turned off to another wing of the house. It would be risky to start methodically barging through each door. If Arkhan were hiding somewhere, he might hear Troxeo and relocate Katie to a new location. He couldn't afford to make a mistake.

Many of the doors had been left open, but a few stood closed. The noise Troxeo heard while down in the entryway had been so muffled that he assumed Katie and Arkhan must be behind one of the closed doors. But which one? There were three on the right and two on the left. He closed his eyes and tried to remember how the house had looked when he was here twenty years ago as a child.

He and Arkhan had scampered through the house, and they were no doubt the ones who had opened some of the doors here and left them that way. He remembered a nursery with tiny furniture and pale colors. He had ventured into a library full of books, printed on wood pulp before electronic storage existed. He remembered a large room with a bed that took up most of the floor and once-grand furniture. The master suite.

There was no equivalent of a master suite in modern Oretoz living. Soldiers bunked at the Fortress or its surrounding buildings, each of them lodged in a private room equal in size to everyone else's. Those who lived with their families further out into the cities reserved modest quarters for themselves with small rooms and simple furniture.

Nothing was as grand and romantic as a master suite, which made it the perfect setting for Arkhan's plans. His cousin hadn't told him of his intentions, but Troxeo knew what he would do. Arkhan would twist Katie's mind until she believed she was in love with him, and she was his eleste.

With complete confidence, Troxeo strode down the hallway toward the closed door at the end. Moving was much easier on a flat surface than it had been going up the stairs, and the pain in his leg subsided enough for him to ignore it. He stepped carefully, watching for weak spots in the floorboards and taking pains to keep his footsteps quiet.

When Troxeo was in front of the door, and his hand rested on the cold metal knob, he stopped. He pressed his ear against the dense wood, desperate to know if Katie was in pleasure or pain. The muffled sounds that he could make out in the hall told him nothing. Blaster at the ready, he turned the knob and shoved the door open.

CHAPTER 26

As Arkhan ripped the remains of Katie's clothes from her body, she was overwhelmed with the feeling that they weren't alone. It was an odd sensation, one that she would have dismissed any other day as mere paranoia. But this was different somehow.

Katie knew that there was no one near them except for the dead squatter, and yet her body was convinced otherwise. It was nothing more than a minute tingling sensation buried deep inside her. She would be lucky if someone else were here. Maybe they would help her get out instead of waiting for sloppy seconds. Instead of talking about her suspicions, she bit her lip instead, which seemed to please Arkhan.

He stared down at Katie's naked body, pleasure evident in his dilated pupils and tight throat. "This is going to be even better than I imagined." He grabbed his shirt with both hands and pulled it over his head.

The door nearly fell off its hinges as it slammed open. Katie screamed, her voice unnaturally loud in the empty house. Arkhan leaped away from the bed to face the door, spreading his feet wide and preparing to do battle.

Troxeo stood in the doorway. Anger and pain pulsed through his features, distorting him into a creature of rage. His blaster was out and at his hip, ready to fire. He looked from Arkhan to Katie and back again, assessing the situation.

He came to save me, she thought. Katie took advantage of Arkhan's distraction and pulled the ragged sheets over her body.

"You've taken my human," Troxeo said to Arkhan, authority in his voice. "You had no right."

Arkhan immediately relaxed when he realized Troxeo had burst in alone and without backup. His cousin didn't make him feel threatened. He now stood with his hands on his hips and a smirk on his face. "I suppose it would have been all right for you to let her rot in prison? At least I'm going to be getting some use out of her now."

Troxeo's fist seemed to come flying across the room. Katie heard the crunch as it smashed into Arkhan's jaw. The dark-haired alien staggered back a step, but he recovered quickly, rubbing the side of his face and resuming his fighting stance.

"If you want to fight, you will lose. You aren't taking the Earthling. Snatch another one." Arkhan barreled toward the doorway, crashing into Troxeo. The two men became a blur of fists.

Katie saw the conflict as an opportunity to escape, but the men were blocking her path to the exit. Although they were distracted with each other, she was sure one of them would grab her as soon as she tried to make a getaway. Considering the way they were fighting, Katie wouldn't have been surprised if they accidentally ripped her in half while trying to decide who deserved to keep the prize.

Scooting up to a sitting position on the old bed, Katie peered out the window behind her. It was a steep drop to the forest floor two stories below. If she went that way, she would injure or kill herself. It was an option, but right now she preferred to be an alive prisoner rather than a free corpse. Frantically, she looked around the room for another way out, but nothing presented itself. She was stuck.

Meanwhile, the two Oretoz had yet to settle their disagreement. Katie thought they were using their mouths too much.

"How are the things I've done any different than what you've done to her?" Arkhan couldn't stop talking as they pounded on each other. "You took her as a prisoner to advance your needs and earn a promotion. I was smarter than you and I took her for myself."

Troxeo landed a solid blow to his cousin's stomach before replying. "I was following orders. I didn't have a choice."

"I doubt the human sees it that way. In her eyes, you aren't any better than I am." Arkhan dodged the next punch.

"How do you know that? I doubt you took the time to talk to her about anything other than how wonderful you are." Troxeo shoved the other man into the doorway. "You probably don't even know her name."

"Do you think you would be doing anything different if you were in my position? I see how you look at her."

Arkhan's fist landed on Troxeo's shoulder as he spoke. "You want her as badly as I do, but you're not man enough to take her."

"Take her?" Troxeo's fist pounded into the other man's nose like a juggernaut, and a crimson river of blood immediately flowed from it. "I'm too much of a man to take her against her will."

Katie looked at Troxeo in confusion. Was there a side to Troxeo she hadn't seen before?

CHAPTER 27

Troxeo took in the scene in the bedroom, at first unable to contemplate what he saw in front of him. Katie had screamed, but that wasn't necessarily because she was frightened of him. She didn't bolt out of the bed and run into his arms, but she wasn't calling Arkhan to defend her, either.

After only a fraction of a second, it no longer mattered to him. In his gut, he could feel what Katie needed, and he knew what he was required to do right now was save her from a monster.

He tossed his blaster behind him. It was no use in confined quarters. A single discharge would be enough to kill all three of them. Troxeo chose another weapon instead, focusing every ounce of his fury as he launched his body at Arkhan. All of his confusion over taking Katie captive and delivering her to the Fortress had been waiting to erupt. Every bit of frustration he felt over trying to find Katie fueled his rage. The edges of his vision were streaked with red as he focused on the fight. His leg burned where the beast had gored him, and he felt a cold trickle of blood as it seeped from the wound. The pain only drove him harder, encouraging Troxeo to push his punches further into his cousin's flesh.

Arkhan's words lit a fire in Troxeo's heart. How dare he try to act as though he was right and everyone else could go to hell? There was no way to justify Arkhan's actions, no matter what he said. It was typical of his cousin to try and talk his way into or out of anything. Troxeo was sick of it. He felt the bones in Arkhan's nose shatter against his knuckles as he plowed his fist into Arkhan's face, giving a satisfying crunch. The other man sagged against the wall behind him and slowly slumped to the floor, finally yielding.

Troxeo turned to look at Katie. She sat on the bed, the scraps of remaining sheets barely covering her nude form. He could tell by her eyes that she was terrified. He came around the edge of the bed until he was at her side, slowly moving so he wouldn't frighten her more. She huddled into herself. Katie's legs were drawn up, and her arms crossed over her chest. Her lower lip quivered as she watched him approach.

"I'm not here to hurt you," he whispered. He reached out a tentative hand and touched her arm.

The second his skin made contact with hers, he knew the truth about their connection. A burst of energy pulsed through his body. He could feel it in his core, and the source was inside the human's body. She was his eleste. They were meant to be together. Now he had to help clear up any misconceptions.

Katie noticed the current of electricity between them as well, jumping as he touched her arm. It wasn't possible for her blue eyes to get any wider, but they softened as she thought about Troxeo's touch and what it might mean.

Arkhan groaned from his position on the floor. His eyes were beginning to blacken, and blood coated his chest and stomach. He tentatively put his hands on his face. He didn't look like he would be getting up soon.

Troxeo turned to Katie and held out his hand. "Let's get you out of here."

She eyed him warily and refused to take it. "Where are you taking me?" Her words bit into the stuffy air of the room. "The last time I went off blindly with someone, it didn't turn out so well. I don't want to go back to the Fortress."

He shook his head. Of course she thought he was going to take her back to prison. That was where he had put her in the first place, wasn't it? He had referred to her as his prisoner again just a moment ago. Troxeo felt like an idiot. "We're going to my ship, and we'll go far away from here. I don't know where yet."

She looked from his outstretched hand to his face and back again. "Are you sure you aren't going to turn me in?"

"I won't."

"How do I know I can trust you?" Katie looked up at him through her voluminous lashes, studying his face carefully. She looked beautiful, and he hoped he would be able to continue to bask in her beauty forever.

Troxeo furrowed his brow in concentration. He had done nothing other than defeat Arkhan to earn her trust at this point. "You don't know with your mind," he replied. "But look in your heart."

His simple words seemed to be enough for her. She put her tiny hand into his, allowing him to pull her up off the bed. She lost her balance as her feet hit the wooden floor, and he caught her in his arms. As she looked up at him, the horror and embarrassment in her face quickly mutated into something else.

"Oh," Katie said, as though she had come to a sudden realization. Their touch felt electric.

Troxeo felt it, too, but he knew they had to get going. He couldn't risk Arkhan regaining consciousness or letting the wound on his leg go untreated for much longer. There was also a possibility that someone had followed him from the Fortress.

Looking down at the torn vestiges of her bodysuit, which lay scattered on the floor and over the bed, he pulled off the cleanest sheet he could find. With a flick to shake off the dust, Troxeo wrapped it around Katie's body and scooped her up into his arms. She flung her hands around his neck, and he could have sworn she was leaning into his chest. He carried her down the stairs and outside. Her skin felt warm and soft against his body.

"I'm strong enough to walk," she insisted as they headed into the woods. Troxeo's only response was to hold her more tightly.

When they reached his ship, he took her to his cabin. It was the largest room and had more luxurious accommodations than the room in which he had initially put her. "I'm going to get the engines going," he explained, watching her carefully for any signs that she was ready to run. "You can get cleaned up and come to the bridge when you're ready."

Carrying her on the way to the ship hadn't been enough for him. He needed to touch her again and feel the smoothness of her skin under his rough hands. But it wasn't the time, and he knew it. Instead, he turned on his heel and headed for the captain's chair. He would get them off the ground and out of the atmosphere, and figure things out from there.

CHAPTER 28

Katie watched the door slide closed behind Troxeo. She stood for a moment in the center of the room, feeling bewildered and wondering what had just happened. With Troxeo's help, she had gotten away from Arkhan. That was the most important thing right now. But what was the sensation that rushed through her body whenever Troxeo touched her? It had affected her very core, changing her from the inside out.

The feeling hadn't only been in her head because she had seen something on his face as well. But what did it mean?

Shaking the questions out of her head, Katie looked at the room around her. The bed here was double the size of the one Troxeo had initially assigned to her. The room was bigger in general, with a side compartment that she instantly recognized as a bathroom. The shower was different from what she was used to on Earth. She randomly pressed buttons underneath the square shower head until the water adjusted to the right temperature and started humming under the spray of warm water.

Katie had only been away from Earth for a few days, but it seemed as though she hadn't bathed in a month. Not seeing a washcloth close by, she ran her hands over her body in an attempt to clean away everything that had happened to her. Another button push released a cascade of foam over her curves, building to a delightful lather.

As she washed, Katie thought about the huge man who had both captured and saved her and was now flying her to safety. She imagined his hard muscles rippling as he used the same shower she occupied. Katie couldn't help but envision the two of them sensually entwined under the steamy water.

Nope. No matter what she thought she was beginning to feel, the Oretoz soldier surely didn't see her that way.

As soon as Katie stepped out of the shower, she started drying herself with a towel she retrieved from the shelf. A quick search of the cabinets in the room revealed a limitless supply of the black sleeveless shirts and olive green pants that were Troxeo's standard attire as well as several pairs of heavy boots. There didn't seem to be any of the tight bodysuits Chixo could produce at the wave of a hand. Katie hoped Chixo had been able to make it back to the Fortress safely.

With no better option to clothe herself, Katie took a robe from a hook by the shower and wrapped it around her body. It was too big for her and sized for an Oretoz male. She had to wrap the belt twice around her slim waist to keep it from trailing on the floor. Unlike the fuzzy fleece robe she left behind on Earth, this one was made of a smooth material similar to the bodysuits. It was slightly thicker than what she was used to, but it still clung to her curves in a flattering way that no robe from Earth could ever achieve.

Katie stepped tentatively out of the room, discovering that the electronic pad next to the door still didn't respond to her fingers. Finding Troxeo was easy. The bridge was just down the hall from her room. She padded quietly up behind him. His wide shoulders rippled as he manipulated the controls in front of him.

The large window on the bridge revealed a deep blackness filled with stars. The slate-blue orb of Oretoz was quickly fading away from the ship. When she took a shower, she missed the takeoff and any turbulence as they left the atmosphere. Perhaps the air was thinner on Troxeo's planet, or perhaps his ship was so advanced that she didn't feel any acceleration.

"Hi."

Troxeo swiveled in his chair. His green eyes swept over her, taking in her damp hair and the robe wrapped around her body. His muscles stiffened visibly, though he made no move to get up.

"I hope it was okay for me to take this robe," she stammered. "It was all I could find in there."

"It's fine. I'm sorry I don't have anything better to offer you." Troxeo cleared his throat uncomfortably.

"I've set a course for Earth. It'll take some time to get there, but we should be well out of the Fortress's sensor range already."

Katie looked down at Troxeo, realizing this was the first time she had the opportunity to be higher than him. He had always towered over her whenever they interacted with each other. Now he was forced to look up at her. The change in position gave him an aura of vulnerability that she found incredibly endearing. She had seen a side of him that was capable of breaking down doors and fighting, but his appearance now made her realize he possessed facets to his personality.

"I want to thank you," she said meekly, not sure if this was the kind of thing that would offend an Oretoz soldier. "I don't know what I would have done if you hadn't come along. Well, I do know, and it shouldn't be mentioned in polite company."

Troxeo shook his head, waving off her thanks. "I just did what was necessary."

"No, I mean what I'm saying." Katie stepped closer to Troxeo and laid her hand over his where it rested on the arm of the chair. Their touch made sparks shoot through her so fiercely that she imagined she could see them, blue and bright where their skin touched. She looked from their hands up into his eyes, wondering if he had felt anything too.

Before Katie had a chance to question herself, she leaned down and pressed her lips to his. They were soft and giving but firm underneath, just like Troxeo himself. It was immediately obvious to her that it was not a simple kiss of thanks for either one of them. It was far more.

His lips answered hers, and her mouth parted, allowing his tongue to probe into her. Katie's hands closed around the back of his neck, running over the prickly stubble where his hair was extremely short. His arms responded in kind, wrapping around her waist and pulling her into his lap. She curled up on top of him, deepening the kiss as thrills of energy continued to run through her body.

"I'm sorry," Troxeo said suddenly, pulling away. "I shouldn't have done that. You've been fighting to get away from men like me, and I have no right to take advantage of you."

Katie looked at his face, but he wouldn't look back at her. She could see a conflict fighting inside of him, and now it was her turn to save Troxeo. "Don't you dare be sorry," she commanded.

"What?" This time, he did look at her with questions in his eyes.

"I want you, Troxeo. I want you more than I ever imagined I could want an Earth man."

"Are you sure?" he whispered.

Katie didn't answer with words, using her body instead. She pressed her lips back to his, skimming his teeth with her tongue. Growling, he wrapped his arms underneath her ass and hoisted her out of the chair. Without breaking the kiss, he carried her back to his room, his cock pressing into her hip. They fell onto the big bed, not bothering to pull back the covers. They didn't want to waste time on anything but each other.

Troxeo was on top of Katie as she ran her hands through his short hair and down his back, pulling at his shirt. He obeyed, pulling himself off her long enough to rip the garment from his body and toss it across the room. As he leaned back down over her, she shoved him away. He looked at her with confusion as she sat up on the bed and pushed him off.

"I told you I wanted you," she explained. "That means I want every part of you."

She moved to the floor and got on her knees, Troxeo standing in front of her. She ran her hands over his bare chest, feeling his rock-like muscles under a scattering of hair. Her hands flowed down to his waistline until she reached his belt buckle. Slowly, teasing him, she pulled his belt apart before gently unzipping his pants. Katie rested her hands on his hips as she ran her fingers against his skin inside his waistband, pushing his clothing down inch by inch. She felt the round firmness of his buttocks as she slid his pants down further until his cock stood in full glory in front of her.

The girls on the spaceship that took her from Earth had speculated about sex with an alien, wondering if their parts would be any different. They had joked about blue erections and giggled frantically. If she ever saw them again, which wasn't likely, she would tell them that there wasn't anything funny about it. His cock thrummed as it pointed at her, eager for events yet to come.

She took it in one hand, feeling the velvety smoothness of skin stretching tautly over it. Unable to resist, she wrapped her lips around his cock, flicking her tongue gently against the tip. Troxeo groaned, and she plunged him further into her mouth. There was no greater turn on than knowing her mate was aroused. She slid her lips toward the base of his shaft, opening her throat to make room for all of him. Katie clutched his butt with one hand and ran her thumb around the base of his balls with the other.

Troxeo hissed as she consumed him, rolling her tongue over his cock and sucking hard as she pulled back. He tangled his hands in her hair, pressing his hips into the pleasure she gave him. A tingling sensation vibrated between her legs, jealous of the attention her mouth was getting. It wouldn't be long before she needed him inside of her.

As though reading her mind, Troxeo pulled himself out of her mouth and tipped her chin up. She had to look at him. "Stop. No more. You've got to let me have a turn now."

CHAPTER 29

Troxeo burned inside after what Katie had done to him. He thought he had known pleasure in his brief encounters with Oretoz women. They had sated themselves quickly and moved on. It was nothing like the exquisite torture Katie wanted to put him through. Her moves were new to him.

He had never thought of delaying pleasure, but now that he had experienced it he couldn't imagine living without it. She had brought him to the very edge of an explosion and even seemed to enjoy it. But Troxeo didn't want to be reduced to the receiving end. With every bit of self-control he possessed, he pushed her away from him.

Katie looked up at him. Her lips were red and swollen. Her eyes were both submissive and commanding, begging him to please her. He slowly unbound the belt at the waist of her robe, determined to torture her as much as she had tortured him. But her clothing fell away quickly, falling to the floor into a puddle and revealing the pearlescent glow of her skin.

Troxeo pushed her back on the bed so he could see her full body. Gorgeous round nipples topped the quivering mounds of her breasts in a shade of pale pink that matched her lips. Katie's hair fell around her shoulders in dark waves that were a sharp contrast with her skin. It tapered down to her trim waist, smooth and flat around her navel. Her hips widened out from there, framing her core.

Troxeo fought against the throbbing in his cock that demanded he plunge into Katie immediately. He desperately wanted to feel her walls close around him and finally purge the sensations she incited in him from the moment he saw her. She had given him new ideas, and he'd be damned if he wasn't going to get the chance to try them out.

He climbed on top of her. He kept his weight on his arms to keep from crushing her small frame as he flicked one of her nipples with his tongue. It hardened and stood firm for him, seeming to beg for more. Troxeo took it into his mouth, licking and sucking just as she had done to him. She murmured with pleasure, encouraging him as she wrapped her arms around his head and pulled him closer.

Troxeo moved between her breasts, reveling in the feel of the mounds of flesh against his face. He could die happy here, but he continued to his right to give her other nipple the attention it deserved. The sweet bud was already tempting him, a hard raisin against her skin. He used his tongue to toy with it as he took as much of her breast into his mouth as he could.

Leisurely, he worked his way down her supple stomach, stopping to kiss each one of her hips before moving down to explore the soft folds between her legs. Taking his cue from her, he ran his tongue over her slit. Katie instantly arched her back and spread her legs wider for him.

Troxeo grinned and pushed his tongue deeper, probing into her sex. She tasted warm and sweet as he moved his mouth over her, flicking, licking, and pushing. He knew he had to be doing something right because Katie angled her hips to give him better access. She ran her hands over her breasts as she moaned.

Parting her lips with his left hand, Troxeo gently pushed one finger inside her. She gasped but didn't protest, and he slid it slowly in and out. Her hips undulated in time with his movements. Troxeo slipped a second finger inside, gently pushing her further open. Katie's juices glistened against his skin. She was pleased, but he couldn't be satisfied. Still moving his fingers, he covered her once again with his mouth. Katie drew a sharp breath as his tongue found her center of pleasure.

She murmured something unintelligible as her hips start pulsing against his face. "Yes, right there. Don't stop." He continued his efforts, determined to work her up to the same mindless intensity he felt. Her hands left her breasts and pulled at his hair, locking his mouth to her sex. He sucked the tiny berry that seemed to control her, teasing her to a peak.

Katie screamed, her legs wrapping around him tightly. "Please," she begged. "I need you inside me."

Troxeo pulled away and shook his head. "I need to keep doing this." He flicked his tongue across her clit once more just to see her squirm.

"I can't take any more," she whimpered. "It's too good. Stop teasing me."

Troxeo's heart pounded. He had wanted this woman so badly, and he never thought they would get the chance to be together. Now she was underneath him, begging him to take her. "Tell me more." He didn't mean to increase her agony, but it was a dream come true. He wanted to live it to the fullest.

"Please," she said. "I want to feel your weight on top of me. I need your big, hard cock inside me, pounding into me again and again. I want you so badly I can't stand it." Her hands had returned to her breasts, holding them and rubbing her thumbs over her hard nipples.

Unable to keep Katie waiting any longer, Troxeo immersed himself into her. She felt tight, but he pushed his way inside until he penetrated her completely. He buried the length of his cock inside her pussy, and she writhed underneath him. He felt the ecstasy of her walls quivering around him, but he also felt something more.

The tiny sparks and pulses which passed between them before now curled inside him like coiled wire, their cores melding together. The entire universe seemed to spin within the two of them, as though someone had made the stars and planets for their pleasure.

He saw the spark reflected in her eyes, and he knew once and for all that he was right. She truly was his eleste. Katie belonged with him, and she knew it as well as he did. So few Oretoz still believed it was possible to find a soulmate, but he had proved them all wrong.

He thrust against her, her warmth surrounding him, inviting him, and claiming him. He was home.

CHAPTER 30

Katie stared at the man on top of her. She had been looking for the perfect man and planning her wedding her entire life. The relationship she had with Ben had worked at the time, but she saw everything from a different point of view now. Katie had spent her time on Earth as a young and foolish girl who knew nothing of the universe.

As Troxeo thrust into Katie, she knew her life had changed. Troxeo was showing her there was more to sex than lust. She felt her heart surge toward him and imagined he felt the same way toward her. Their bodies melded together. It didn't matter which planet they came from or what happened between them before this moment.

Katie surrendered herself to life with Troxeo, whatever it brought. She couldn't imagine living any other way. His presence was intoxicating, making her quiver and convulse around him. She wanted him to stay inside her, to fill her up and make her whole.

She shuddered with pleasure, moaning and pressing up against him. Her core rippled around his cock, pulling him further inside. They built up to their climax together, the intensity increasing as they rocked back and forth, exclamations of pleasure growing louder as they became one. Katie screamed, unable to hold anything back anymore. She felt his cock expand inside her, reacting to her pleasure and filling her with his seed.

He collapsed next to her, sweaty and exhausted. She allowed herself a smile of pride that she had been able to bring such a big man to his knees with pleasure. "That was lovely."

Troxeo was too busy trying to catch his breath to respond. He lay on the pillow next to her, gasping and running his hands over his face. He blinked and stared up at the ceiling as though he wasn't sure what had happened, but he nodded dumbly.

"So did you like fucking a human?" She felt confident of her sexual prowess on Earth, but she didn't know what the standards were for the alien. Making love to Troxeo was not the same as it had been with anyone else before. Fucking wasn't even the right word for it. It wasn't anything like what she used to do with Ben. She felt raw passion now. Unleashed, unhinged, and uninhibited.

"Liked it?" Troxeo let out a breathless laugh, a noise that Katie had never heard from him before. "If I had known it could have been like that, I never would have taken you to the Fortress in the first place!"

Now it was Katie's turn to laugh. "That's good to hear. I guess you'll be ready for some more later."

Troxeo rolled over, pinning Katie to the bed with his chest. "I intend to get as much of you as I can before the time comes." He trailed off, his countenance becoming somber. "We only have a few hours remaining before I return you to Earth."

Katie felt like crying out in protest. Although it was true that she had been trying to get back to Earth ever since Troxeo had taken her prisoner, things had changed now. Various schemes flashed through her mind, focused on how she could stay together with Troxeo. Returning to Oretoz was out of the question. They might shoot her on sight when she was recognized as an escaped prisoner. Troxeo was likely a wanted man as well.

She couldn't bring him back to Earth and pretend to live a normal life there either. Though the people on her home planet were aware aliens existed in the universe, it would be unusual for an entirely new race to show up without any fanfare. Katie had likely averted an Oretoz invasion by escaping from Commander Reck. That might change if EarthGov tried to make contact.

Tears welled in Katie's eyes. After a lifetime of waiting, she had found her true love, and he was about to be ripped away from her. "I don't want to leave you, Troxeo. I don't care if I don't make it back to Earth. I need you. I don't know how to make it happen. Can we float around in space forever? Please don't force me to go."

He kissed her on her forehead, a gesture so tender that it only made her tears spill down her face. "I love you, Katie." His voice spoke straight to her heart, cradling it and stabbing it simultaneously.

CHAPTER 31

Rolling back to his side of the bed, Troxeo racked his brain. He knew it would be impossible for them to stay on either of their planets. It would be terrible luck to find a woman he was destined to be with but then have to give her up. Katie was right. They couldn't travel forever without any plans for resupplying.

"I wish there were a place we could go where none of our complications mattered," she whispered. "Some place where neither one of us would be hunted, scrutinized, or dissected. Maybe a place where there aren't any other people at all."

Troxeo listened to her words, imagining a place that would provide a peaceful rest from all they had been through. Suddenly a thought occurred to him that made him want to smack himself for not having realized it sooner. "I think there's a planet that has everything you want."

"Really? Where is it?" She sat up on her elbow to look at him. Her breasts rubbed against his arm, but he forced himself to concentrate on the matter at hand.

"Several years ago, when they promoted me to Captain, the military gave me a bonus. As a soldier bunked in the Fortress, I didn't need any extra money. I could have used it for upgrades to my ship or saved it for my retirement if I was fortunate enough to live that long. Instead, I combined it with some other savings and bought a parcel of land on a distant planet. Mezval is a resort world for wealthy people who want to be left alone. I only visited it long enough to approve the purchase, but I remember it is beautiful. The land I bought is near an ocean, and it's big enough that we would never see our neighbors or know they existed. Better yet, they won't know we exist, either. There's a nebula near the planet that turns the sky purple and green in the early mornings."

"Do you think we could live there safely?" she asked hopefully.

"Definitely. Mezval is practically uninhabited compared to Earth or Oretoz. Commander Reck will never think to look for us there. He has no idea that I bought the land. Nobody does, as a matter of fact. I was too embarrassed to tell anyone."

A smile played at the corners of her lips. The expression was a direct contrast to the tears that still clung like crystals to her eyelashes. "Why?"

He smiled back at her, his humiliation seeming childish. "It's not the kind of activity befitting a soldier. Especially one with rank." Troxeo remembered what made Mezval such an exclusive destination, "This planet is in the cluster of stars you call the Milky Way. It's too far to concern anyone on your planet, but it means we can swing close enough to Earth on the way there to transmit a message to your family. You can let them know you're safe."

"Oh, Troxeo! You must be the sweetest, most thoughtful man in the whole universe! No wonder I had to leave Earth to find you!" She threw her arms around him and smothered his face with kisses.

"I'm warning you, we'll have to find a way to kill time until we get there," he said with a suggestive glance.

"Well, I'm sure we'll come up with something. I already have a few ideas."

"Like what?" He nuzzled her neck, nipping at her tender skin.

"I'm nowhere near being done with you yet. The lather in that shower, for instance, would look fantastic on you." She reached a hand down toward his inner thigh, where he had already begun to harden again.

"Yeah?" He broke away from her neck and moved down to her breasts, pushing them up around his face.

"Oh, yeah. And we've only tried one position so far." She leaned her head back in delight as the stubble on his chin raked against her.

"How many are there?" he asked, his voice muffled by her voluptuousness.

Katie pulled herself out from underneath him and shoved him down, moving on top of him. She straddled Troxeo and impaled herself on his cock. She glided back and forth, tilting her hips and making him touch her in the perfect spot. "Enough."

Troxeo's hands couldn't decide if they wanted to grab at her breasts or fondle her slit as she moved on top of him. Katie was a paradise he had never known could exist. "I can handle multiple positions."

Katie closed her eyes and tipped her head back. She solved the debate of his hands when she licked a finger and rubbed it against herself in slow, methodical circles. "There are many more of them that I can't wait to show you. And one more thing..."

"Yes?" He could feel her tightening around him, and he bucked against her. Her breasts jiggled as she rode him, and he didn't think they would ever make it out of bed.

Katie opened her eyes. "I love you, Troxeo."

If you enjoyed this book, please review it on Amazon! Your review helps me succeed as an author.

To stay up-to-date on my latest releases, sign up for my newsletter at:

http://lisalace.com/newsletter/

OTHER BOOKS BY LISA LACE

WATER WORLD WARRIOR: A TERRAMATES NOVEL

Why would I want to be married to an alien?

I should not have applied to TerraMates! The idea was crazy. I'm a young woman, in the prime of my life.

But I was desperate.

When I landed on another world, his appearance intrigued me. He dripped sexuality and moved like an animal. We have three days together before he sets sail without me. Am I going to escape or submit to my desires?

TAKEN: A TERRAMATES NOVEL

What happens when TerraMates runs out of applicants?

There's never a shortage of wealthy alien bachelors looking for the thrill of mating with a human. They want our women.

But despite the promise of riches, sometimes the pool of available brides runs dry.

How does TerraMates find more girls, and where do they go? When Lyzette gets taken off the street, she finds out.

WATER WORLD CONFIDENTIAL: A TERRAMATES NOVEL

He needed a wife. I wanted an alien lover.

The first time I saw Jori, I hated everything about him. He didn't care about anything except himself. On the other hand, his body was spectacular, and his muscles were firm. I couldn't stop thinking about him.

When TerraMates gave me the chance to marry Jori, I took it. I knew I needed the money. What I didn't know was that Jori's exterior was a facade, and he had kept secrets from everyone his entire life.

ALPHA'S ENSLAVED BRIDE: A TERRAMATES NOVEL

Knowing the future isn't a blessing. It's a curse. Especially when you've seen your death.

I'm going to die in the arms of someone I have never seen before. He's a person I will love, but I don't know anything about him.

When TerraMates matched me with Airik, I couldn't believe it. This sexy alien could see the future, just like me. I wasn't alone anymore. I quickly found out he knows nothing about Earth or humans. I married him, but will I be safe with him?

www.ingramcontent.com/pod-product-compliance
Lightning Source LLC
Chambersburg PA
CBHW020620180626
46810CB00007B/2873

* 9 7 8 0 6 9 2 7 3 6 5 4 8 *